Caroline's Story: Serenity

Finding Herself Series
Book 3

Erica J Whelton

Publisher: Sunseri Design Publishing
ISBN: 978-1-956069-10-5

Printed in the United States of America

As this story is about loss, love, and friendship,
who better to dedicate this to than **all the women**
who have always been there for me.
Thank you for straightening my crown.

Table of Contents

*You may not end up where you thought you were going,
but you will always end up where you were meant to be....*
- Unknown

Chapter One: Present Day

Today, I was babysitting my neighbor, Becca's young children. I was always happy to help her out. She and her children were like the children and grandchildren I'd never had. I loved them dearly.

I smiled at them as the two thumbed through my photos of years gone by. It warmed my heart to see them smiling and happy. We have all come so far.

Missy is a bright, sassy, and curious little girl. She is remarkably mature for her age, and sometimes I almost forget she is only five. A deep thinker who is always observing, she can come up with the best questions.

Davy is a sweet, nearly three-year-old. He is a kindhearted, loving toddler who is very well-behaved. Most children his age push the boundaries and throw tantrums regularly, not Little Davy. He is one of those goes-with-the-flow types.

They have primarily been raised by their older sister, Mandy, who, at eighteen years old, was running a successful and growing cleaning/yardwork business, supervising three employees. As a result, she has more inner strength, maturity, and responsibility than some people twice her age.

Honestly, she reminds me a lot of myself, though it took me longer to mature to her level. It is incredible as she was born to a young mother and did not have the most stable home life until recently.

Their mother, Rebecca Walker, was the only daughter of my longtime neighbors and good friends Wade and Elizabeth Walker. They had tried for years to have a baby, and they finally had Becca.

She had been a quiet, sweet child until around age thirteen, when she started hanging around a group of older kids. They were doing all the stereotypical troubled teen things, skipping school, drinking, and smoking. So, she started wearing heavy, dark make-up and tight clothing.

Not at all like a 13-year-old girl should be acting or dressing and not one raised by Wade and Beth Walker, two of our most prominent citizens of Glenn Lake.

But, then again, sometimes folks didn't always know what happened behind closed doors. She had rebelled in the way most girls might in her situation. I knew some of what went on simply because of proximity to their house. I had only learned about her life behind that closed door in recent months.

She became pregnant with Mandy at only fourteen. My heart ached for her because she was nowhere near ready for the responsibility of a baby. She could barely care for herself and had no idea what life was like or how much a baby would change it.

But mostly, I ached for the baby I lost and those I never had the chance to have. It was just unfair to see someone so young have what I lost and not even know what a true blessing having a child was. Instead, she saw it as a curse.

Wade and Beth were so upset with Becca that they kicked her out of the house. I disagreed with their method, especially after they had tried so hard to have her, but I just kept that to myself. There was nothing worse than a nosy neighbor interfering in family business though I did offer Becca a place to stay.

But I couldn't see her and a baby out on the streets. She declined, saying her parents were too close. I could understand that, but I wanted that baby to be safe.

So, I gave her some money which of course she took. Would she spend it foolishly or wisely? I would never know, but I wanted to help her. I wouldn't be able to look myself in the face if I hadn't at least offered.

"My door is always open to you and the baby."

"Thank you, Ms. Graham; you have always been so sweet to me." She had said.

We hugged, and she was gone.

Time and a lot of changes brought her back to Glenn Lake, and that's how today, her two youngest children and I were sifting through my old photos.

I had years and years' worth from my 72 years of life. They were somewhat organized into decorative boxes or photo albums.

Looking through them always brought back a mix of feelings; the good, the bad, and the ugly.

"Is this you, Grammy? Is this you?" Missy snapped me out of my daydream. I looked at the picture she was waving at me.

"It is, sweetheart."

"You are so beautiful!"

"Beautiful, Grammy!" Little Davy echoed.

"What about this one?" As she shoved another picture in my face, only an inch from my eyes. I chuckled and gently pulled her hand back so I could see it.

"Yes, that's me too. This was taken when I lived in New York City. I was, oh gosh, let me think, 19 or 20 years old."

Walter had taken this picture. It must have been close to when he was shipped off to Vietnam.

"You lived in New York City? Like where they have the Thanksgiving parade." I nodded in reply. She clapped. "Wow! What was it like?"

I didn't know how to answer her. It was fantastic, exciting, and the happiest I had been in my life, at least at first when it was Walter and me, though, once he was gone?

Well, goodness, how could I tell her how awful life had gotten? How lonely? How every street and every restaurant reminded me of him? How do you explain finding the love of your life only to lose them way too soon and then never finding that passion or devotion in another person?

To a 5-year-old, the world is still a big, safe, innocent place. Granted, she had seen some scary things in her short life, but she had been somewhat sheltered thanks to Mandy and trusted that her sister would always protect her. Still, she wouldn't understand how unfair life could be.

Not that my time there was all awful, but just too many reminders to stay. Also, the moment I stepped foot in Glenn Lake, it felt like I had finally come home.

I decided it was best to keep it simple and talk about the positives. The Daileys were the only ones who knew about my past. It wasn't a part of my life that I thought about much.

"It was busy and full of people. But there was always something fun going on. Lots of restaurants, plays to attend, parties. Someone playing music in the park or on the street corners. It was... fun."

Fun but not enough of a distraction from my heartache. Even working countless hours hadn't helped push the ghosts from my mind or heart.

"That sounds amazing! Why would you leave?"

Her questions always caught me off guard, but she kept me on my toes and my mind sharp.

"I just needed a change of scenery. A fresh start. Texas sounded like a wonderful place for that, plus my best friends the Daileys moved here, so I followed them." I smiled at her, hoping that was a good enough explanation.

"Oh, I love the Daileys but... but what does change of scenery mean?"

"It just means that... Well, you know how you and Davy play in your backyard most of the time. You are happy there, but sometimes you come to play in my yard. Why do you do that?"

"Because we love you."

"Aw, well, I love you both too. But you sometimes do that because I have a different backyard than you do. You know, like I have the big tree you both like to play under."

"Oh yeah. Okay, so you wanted to go play somewhere else."

"Yes, except I liked it so much, I stayed. It became my new home."

"I think I understand." She picked up another picture and thankfully changed the subject, "Oh, look at this picture! This is such a pretty dress."

"Thanks, this is called an empire dress. It was fashionable back then."

"Knock, knock..." It was Becca back from her counseling session. She had been in counseling for nearly two months now.

She was a recovering alcoholic and not that long ago hit rock bottom when she was in a terrible car accident. It was the reality check she had needed to get her life on track again. I was so happy to see her getting on a better path for herself and her children.

"Hello, dear. We are just looking at old pictures." I said as I picked up another stack of fading pictures. The kids smiled in greeting but kept looking through the photos.

"Oh well, that's fun. Anything good in there?"

"Oh yes, mama, we saw a bunch of Grammy, and did you know she lived in New York City?"

"I did know that actually," Becca said as she sat on the floor with us, grabbing a few pictures. Davy climbed into her lap.

"She wanted a change of scenery, so she moved here," Missy said with an emphasis on change of scenery.

Becca and I exchanged a smirk as we both stifled a giggle at her big words. Becca knew I had taught Missy that phrase, but in typically Missy fashion, she understood and remembered everything.

"We are lucky she did so she can be part of our family," Becca said.

"Yeah..." Both kids said together.

"Oh, well, dear, I feel like the lucky one." I really did feel blessed, especially at times like this, "Let me see, I think I might have some pictures of you around here somewhere."

"Oh gosh, nobody wants to see those! Do you?" She smiled at her kids.

"I do! I do!"

"Me too, Mama, me too!" Little Davy bounced around and clapped.

We dug through some of the pictures as I tried to find the ones I had in mind.

"Here we go. You are about Davy's age here."

"Oh Mama, you look so, so cute. Look at your curly hair! Just like mine!" Missy said, bouncing her curls in her palm.

"Mama, is dat you?"

"Yes, that's me, sweetie. I was about your age in this picture. Wow, I didn't realize how much he favors me. I always thought he looked more like Jimmy."

"Oh, and here you are about Missy's age," I said, handing her another picture.

We looked at pictures for another hour. Laughing, reminiscing, and telling stories to the children. It was a wonderful afternoon, even if the memories were sure to haunt me for the next several days or possibly weeks.

"Well, we better head home. Let me help you clean these up before we go." Becca offered and started stacking up pictures to put back in their boxes.

"Oh, don't worry about it, dear. I'm going to look through them for a while longer." I said, standing so I could walk them to the door.

My joints protested just enough to remind me of my age. After looking at the photos, it was easy to forget I wasn't still in my 20s. I tried not to let it show in my face.

"Okay. Thanks for watching them." Becca said as she hugged me goodbye.

"Anytime, anytime. I love having them." I smiled at Missy and Davy.

"Thank you, Grammy!" Missy hugged me tightly. Then little Davy followed his sister's example.

"I love you, Grammy." He whispered.

My heart fluttered. This little boy was an old soul and knew I needed to hear that. I watched them from my porch as they walked to their house next door. Missy and Davy holding their mama's hands and telling her all about their day. It was a sweet sight.

After Becca and the kids left, I sat in my favorite high-backed club chair with a hot cup of tea, trying to fight the memories that I knew were coming. It didn't help. I could fight all I wanted, but my mind pulled them up as if I was watching a movie, remembering it all like it was yesterday. This happened whenever I looked through my old pictures. I am not sure how I let Missy talk me into looking at them.

Even after all this time, roughly fifty years, thoughts of him still brought tears to my eyes and that deep ache in my chest.

I didn't even need to look at the hidden box of pictures. Those were so precious and too painful to look at it, but I kept them anyway.

I could almost hear his voice and the unique way he said my name. I'd get goosebumps as he would whisper my name, and then he'd pull me into his warm embrace and give me a toe-curling kiss. The strength of his arms and the smell of his soap made me feel so safe, as if I were home.

I sometimes dream of being right there in his arms. Safe and loved and no longer alone.

Chapter Two: November 1965 - May 1967

I first met Walter Franks in high school. I was a freshman; he was a junior. Star football player, on the student council, and all-around good guy. Loved by student and teacher alike.

Along with most of the girls in our school, I had a massive crush on him. But unfortunately, he never noticed me.

I tried my best to be in just the right place at the right time to get noticed. I always wore my most fashionable clothing, and, between classes, I would go out of my way to be outside his locker or near his classroom.

Sometimes I'd get lucky, and he'd smile at me with that one dimple, his deep brown eyes sparkling. I'd swoon into a girlfriend or the wall, whatever was nearby. He was to die for gorgeous.

But it wasn't until my sophomore year that I talked to him for the first time. I was hovering near his locker, pretending to talk to my friend, Dottie.

"Hey, you're Caroline, right?" He said.

"That's me."

"Right, right. So, the winter formal is coming up in a few weeks, got a date?"

"Not yet."

"Well, would you want to go with me?"

"Yes, that would be great." I tried to keep my voice calm and even. Dottie made a slight squeal but reeled herself back in quickly.

"Great. I'll get with ya soon for the details."

"Sounds good." I smiled.

He nodded and walked away.

Once he was out of earshot, Dottie and I melted into a fit of giggles. I couldn't believe my luck.

When I got home that afternoon, I rushed in to tell my mom.

"It finally happened," I said, grabbing a fresh-baked cookie from the plate she was still filling.

"What?" She asked with a smile as she pretended to swat my hand away from the cookies.

"Walter Franks talked to me, and not just talked to me, but he asked me to the winter formal."

"Oh, that is wonderful!" She beamed, "You'll need a dress, and I think I have the perfect pattern."

Over the next few weeks, we worked on my dress. My mother was a whiz with the sewing machine. She could whip up the most elegant creations or the most fashion-forward pieces. She made almost all my clothes, and I was known for being on trend with the latest style.

Because I wanted this to be the first of many dates with Walter, so this dress had to be perfect.

My mother really outdid herself, creating an ice blue floor-length dress with bishop sleeves and a high waist. We paired it with a delicate lace flower belt. I could just picture myself standing with Walter for pictures or dancing around the floor with him.

As I modeled it for my mother to make the last adjustments, I pictured how the night would go. All the girls would be green with envy, and all the boys wishing they were in Walter's place.

Walter had solidified plans for our date, and we'd spoken between classes a few times. I never knew what to say to him, but he was sweet and funny, helping to steer the conversation enough that I didn't have to think about topics. He was quick with a joke and smiled all the time. His single dimple made my knees weak.

When it was finally the night. I dressed with such care, ensuring my hair was styled perfectly, my make-up was simple but elegant, and my dress was smoothed and fit like a glove. I stared at myself in the full-length mirror.

"Perfect," I said.

I watched from my bedroom window as he pulled up. He looked handsome in his dark gray suit as he walked from his car up our long sidewalk to the front door. I let my parents greet him before I ascended the stairway of our Victorian Styled house.

"Oh, my, Caroline," Walter said put a hand to his chest, "You will be the most beautiful lady there."

"Why, thank you." I blushed.

He fastened a corsage to my dress. The pale pink carnation and rose were accented with baby's breath, and a hot pink ribbon tied it all together. He had asked my favorite color, so it was no surprise that he had gotten it right.

As I walked into the dance on the arm of Walter Franks, it was just as I imagined. I could feel all the girls staring. They were definitely jealous. I, just a sophomore, was here with the high school sweetheart. All the guys wanted to be him; all the girls wanted to be with him.

Sorry, girls, this guy is all mine, at least for the night. I thought as he led me straight on the dance floor.

"I'm so glad you said yes." He whispered as he put his arm around me.

"I'm so glad you asked," I replied, fighting a giggle.

We danced to nearly every song, only taking breaks to grab a cup or two of punch. He was a perfect gentleman and was attentive to all my needs.

When it was time to go, I was somewhat sad. I wanted this night to go on forever. I could have spent an eternity in his arms. It felt like safety, comfort, and coming home. But, of course, I didn't confess this to him; after all, it was only one date and no promise of a second.

At his car, he held the door open until I was in. We didn't speak much on the drive back to my house. But, as we got close, he switched off his headlights and rolled to stop in front of my house.

"I had a wonderful time with you, Caroline." He said, turning towards me.

"I did too. Thank you."

"I'd like to see you again."

"I'd love that." My stomach fluttered.

"May I kiss you?"

"Yes," My throat instantly dry as he leaned towards me.

The kiss, my first, was mind-blowing, knock your socks off kind of kiss. There were a few more before we finally said goodnight.

From that day on, we became nearly inseparable. Every Friday and Saturday night, we had a standing date.

We'd go to the drive-in or bowling with our friends. We spent so much time at the local diner, we had a special booth, and the waitress knew our order.

Then after church on Sundays, we alternated having lunch with either his family or mine. After which, we'd spend the afternoon together.

At school, he always walked me to class, carrying my books. It was all like a dream. I was so proud walking in the hallway with Walter Franks escorting me.

Sadly, the school year ended, and he was going to university in the Fall. It would be several hours away. I thought for sure he would end things between us, but he had other plans.

"I know you will meet someone new and forget all about me," I said, choking on my tears.

"Oh, no, sweetheart, never. You are my soul mate, and I plan to marry you one day."

"You do?"

"Oh yes, I knew it from the first moment we spoke." He wiped a tear with his thumb, "So, no tears, okay?"

"But I don't want to say goodbye."

"It will go by so fast; you won't even have time to miss me." He kissed my forehead and then made me promise to trust him. I did.

I tried to be upbeat and cheery, but with him away, I was moody, and it became hard to focus. My only bright spot was when he would call me. We had a set date every Thursday evening. It was the only time he had a break from football and studies.

He would tell me all about the school, his classes, new friends. It all sounded so wonderful.

"You have a different life there," I said.

"Kind of, but it isn't the one I want." He chuckled, "When you graduate, I think we should move to New York City."

"What? That's ... how?"

"We'll get jobs and an apartment. Think about Caroline, we could be together. Every day we'd be together."

I did think about it every single day until I graduated. Then, the week before my graduation, he came home. His semester had ended, and he was here to watch my graduation ceremony.

"I did it. I got a job in New York," he said, picking me up in his arms and swinging me around. "Our dreams can come true now."

He would be working in a mailroom at some big corporation on Wall Street.

"It's not the best job, but it's a start. I'll work my way up." He was so full of confidence. I giggled.

"I guess I'll need to find something now too!" I beamed. I couldn't wait for our next adventure, and we would be together. "But now we have to tell our parents."

"No, problem." He beamed, "We'll ask them to go out to dinner. That new Italian place, maybe."

"Alright." A public place meant less yelling, I hoped. Though knowing my parents, it would be silence and guilty stares.

I was so nervous the day of our big reveal. I paced around. I was jumpy, especially when my mother spoke to me.

"What is wrong with you today, Caroline?" My mother asked after the fifth time she startled me, just by existing, "You seem anxious. Are you getting sick?" Her eyes went right to my abdomen.

"Mom, no." I stomped my foot, "Why do you think *that*?"

"No, no, I don't." She stuttered, "I just know that you and Walter asked us all to dinner tonight, so I thought, ... well, something big was happening."

I simply nodded. I couldn't lie to my mother. As much as I wanted to reassure her that nothing was happening, I knew that wasn't true. Of course, they weren't going to be thrilled with my life choice, but that's the point; it's my life.

Finally, it was time for dinner. We arrived at the restaurant, just moments before the Franks.

When Walt got out of the car, our eyes locked, and a huge grin formed on his face as he strode straight to me. He took my breath away every time I saw him, even after two years together. I hoped I never lost that feeling for him.

Our parents greeted each other, and then we headed in. It was uneventful until Walter cleared his throat halfway through the meal.

"Mom, Dad. Mr. and Mrs. Graham, thank you for meeting us. Caroline and I have something to tell you."

"Oh, you're getting married!" His mom squealed, and everyone looked down at my left hand. No ring.

"Um, no, well, not yet." He looked over at me and winked, "For now, we are going to move in together ... and move to New York City. I've already secured a job there."

My mother looked at me before she started rapidly fanning herself but didn't say a word. She now knew why I'd been jumpy and edgy all day. My father shoved more food in this mouth, making no eye contact with me.

The Franks, on the other hand, started rapid-firing questions.

"What will people think?" His father said, "That's not traditional. That's simply not done."

"Well, they can think what they want. We do plan to get married but on our time schedule."

"What about college?" His dad asked.

"How will you make a living without finishing your education?" His mother added.

Walt had an answer for everything, explaining his whole plan.

"I got the job in the mailroom for now, but they told me I could easily work my way up."

"It's so dangerous. There were all those riots a few years ago, then the transportation strike last year." His dad said.

Being from our quiet town, I am sure this all did seem scary to them, but I was excited by the mystery and adventure of this new city. Plus, I would get to live with Walter and not have to say goodbye to him.

"We'll be fine. I talked to a few buddies at school. They know the area and told me everyone is moving to either the Upper East Side or the Upper West Side." He said, "I already have arranged for a couple of appointments to see a few apartments. We'll just need to be there by Tuesday."

I looked at my parents. My dad stopped chewing mid-bite but didn't say anything. While my mother continued fanning herself, only stopping for a moment here or there as she processed the conversation.

"How will you afford rent? You haven't started work yet."

"I have some money saved from doing odd jobs. It should be enough to get us started." Walt answered.

I beamed at his grace and composer during this conversation. Though I was not nearly as confident.

He had told me that he'd saved about $200. I had a little bit myself from babysitting and gifts from graduation, so we should be okay for a brief time.

Of course, we'd both have to work to make this happen, but I was willing and ready, especially if it meant being with Walt.

"I also plan to sell my car. We wouldn't need it once we get to the city. That should give us more than enough to get started." Walter added.

The three of them talked and talked while my parents barely looked at me. They had hoped I would go to a university and get my degree. I still could but in New York.

"Well, it sounds like you have thought of everything." His dad finally said.

"I think we have," Walt said, reaching for my hand, "Mr. and Mrs. Graham, I hope we have your blessing."

My dad finally looked up. He glanced at us both for a moment or two, then sighed.

"Nothing I say is going to change that girl's mind." He winked at me. My mother stared at him, but after a second, she nodded and flashed a weak smile.

With that, it was settled. Walt and I were moving to New York City and could start our future together.

Chapter Three: June 1967

Over the next few days, we packed up our few belongings and finalized our travel plans. Since we'd be driving, he had it mapped out, including the gas mileage for the car so he could plan our stops.

"And you see, I have the map all marked. We should be stopping about here," He pointed to a blue dot he'd placed on the map, "for gas, and here for food."

I studied that map, memorizing our route, imagining the scenery. It would mean hours together with just me and Walter. This was such a huge step, and I couldn't be more excited. This was the biggest thing I'd ever done in my life.

Granted, I was only eighteen and still had a lot of life to get through. But this was just the beginning.

Both his parents and mine gave us additional money so we could easily survive for three to four months with what we had if we were careful and budgeted. Then if we got jobs and sold the car, we should be set.

He would start his job within days of us arriving. Then once we were settled, I'd start looking for one.

My mother had barely spoken to me since we announced our plans. But tonight, as I was preparing for my last night in my childhood bed, she came to my room.

"Caroline, may I come in?" She said from the doorway.

"Yes, of course." I sat up on my bed.

"I just ... I just wanted to tell you how brave I think you are. This is scary, so much change and to a big city. Living with a man." She dabbed her eyes with a tissue. Something mom was always good for, having a tissue when it was needed, "I was never so brave."

"Oh, mama, you are. Look at all you have done."

"No, no. I didn't leave home until I married your father, and I don't regret that. However, I would have loved to have done something adventurous, daring. Instead, I got right to being a wife and then soon after a mother. Again, things I don't regret, but... well, I'm only glad you are going to have a little fun first."

"You can still have adventures. You're done raising children and can travel now, take up a new hobby, and you can come to visit me, and we will go to all the trendy, groovy places."

She laughed, "It's a deal."

We hugged and then sat up, talking about life and love. We laughed, we cried. It was the perfect send-off for both of us.

The following day, Walt arrived before the sun to begin our drive to our new home.

"Ready?"

"I am." I hugged my parents, only a few tears were shed. Then we were off.

It was a long drive, but we enjoyed every minute. Singing to the radio and talking about our future. I almost hated for this part to be over, but I was ready to stretch my legs.

So, when the skyline came into view, my body hummed with excitement. The tall buildings came closer and closer into view.

"We are here. We are finally here!" I did a little dance in my seat.

"Ready to start this next chapter together?" He asked, taking my hand.

"I am. You?"

"Oh, yeah." He pulled my hand to his lips, kissing the back of it, sending goosebumps up and down my body.

We made our way through the crowded streets to the cheap hotel we had booked for the week, give, or take. Our stay here would depend on how quickly we found an apartment.

We parked our car along the street near the hotel and loaded our few possessions into the room. Although we didn't have a lot, the boxes and luggage filled the tiny room.

"I knew the rooms here would be smaller than we are used to, but we are going to be tripping over boxes all week," I said, stepping over one to make my way to the bed.

"It's temporary. We'll find our own place in no time." He smiled, "Want to go explore?"

"Yes!"

We were on the Upper West Side, and as we walked, it was clear this was not our sleepy little bedroom town. There were people and movement everywhere, and there seemed to be music coming from every direction. The music was only mildly drowned out by the cars and the voices of people.

We got right into the flow of things and followed it to restaurants, shopping, and bars.

"Walt, this is incredible." I couldn't seem to take it all in fast enough. The people, the sights, the smells. It was all new, and everywhere I looked, there was something else to see.

"It is." He squeezed my hand.

We explored our new corner of the world for a few more hours before exhaustion took over, and we headed back to our room.

We showered together. After which, we collapsed into bed; though my body was tired, the rest of me was too excited to sleep and mildly embarrassed. I'd never slept in a bed with a man before. But, this was going to be different.

"Good night, sweetheart." He whispered in the dark.

"Good night, my love."

He reached for my hand, and that's how we slept. Hand in hand and ready for this adventure together.

The following day, we had our appointments to see a few apartments. I hardly slept the night before as I kept mentally pinching myself. I was in a city living with Walter Franks, my once high school crush, and we were starting our new life together.

I dressed with great care for our day. However, from our outing last night, I knew I would have to change up my wardrobe quite a bit. Going from my hometown, where I had always been known for being stylish, to here where my clothing seemed childish and outdated.

As I buttoned my peach-colored blouse and fastened my plaid skirt, it was going to have to do for until I could shop for updated, hip clothing.

Once dressed, I tried to style my hair like the other girls here, but it didn't work quite right. I'd need a cut to get it to style correctly.

"Oh, well," I said to my reflection, "I still think I look pretty good."

"You do, darlin', you sure do," Walt said, putting his arms around me and kissing my neck.

"Aw, thanks,"

We headed out for our first appointment. I couldn't wait to see where we might live. It would be my first time living away from home.

Stepping out of the hotel, I noticed the daytime vibe was much different from the evening one. Everyone looked as though they had somewhere important to be. Last night everyone had been dressed to the nines, and there had been more of a party atmosphere.

Today, everyone was professionally dressed. Men in their single-breasted grey, black, or navy suits with a crisp white shirt and a simple tie. They looked ready to take on the day.

Many of the women also wore a type of suit, either with a skirt or pants with colors varying from dark grays and blues to reds, greens, purples, and everything in between.

Our first appointment was in a dark red brick building with chipped stone steps. We stepped into a small lobby with tile floors that were so dingy you couldn't tell what color they were supposed to be, and the walls had peeling, yellowed paper. The whole room smelled like burnt food, body odor, and smoke. Not a welcoming, home-like feeling. I couldn't imagine coming home each day to this.

An old, worn-out man came from a side door with a cloud of smoke following him.

"Are you Walter?" He asked, pointing his cigarette at us.

"I am, and this is –" Walter said, but the man cut him off.

"This way."

He led us up the narrow stairs to the third floor. We went to the end of the hallway, and he opened the fourth door on the left.

"Here ya go." He pushed the door open and gestured for us to go in.

The smell of dust, mold, and more cigarette smoke wafted out at us. It burned my eyes, but despite the smell, we went inside. It was a 10-foot by 10-foot room with two doors on the far wall. On the left wall was a kitchen area with the bare necessities; a tiny refrigerator, a two-burner stovetop with an oven, and a sink.

"Bathroom and closest there. This is the livin' room, kitchen, and bedroom." The man gestured.

"I see. And you said this is $90 a month?" Walt asked.

"That's right."

I opened the bathroom door to find a room I could barely turn around in. The sink and tub had rust stains, the enamel was chipping, and there were missing tiles on the floor, revealing the subfloor.

I knew I'd need to lower my standards. This wasn't my family home anymore. We were in the big city, and it was a different life. Despite knowing that, I turned towards Walt and shook my head.

"Well, sir, we thank you for your time. We'll let you know."

"Alright, but no guarantee it will still be available. As fast as new people are comin' in here, I can't keep these long."

"I understand, and thank you for your time."

We followed him back downstairs and then back out to the street.

"I knew it wouldn't be perfect, but it would take me weeks to clean that enough to live in," I said.

"We have more to look at, and I'm sure we'll find a place."

The next place was marginally better, but the rent was a bit more. Like the story of the three bears, though, the third place was the perfect fit.

It was on the fourth floor, which I didn't like, but it was perfect in almost every other way. The rent was $100 a month, and it had an actual bedroom. The kitchen and living room were combined, but that was expected. The bathroom was typical, with a small basin sink, toilet, a shower, and two narrow shelves for storage, but not much else.

The whole apartment would still take a while to clean, but at least it was a bit larger than the others. Plus, we could still afford it.

"You can move in by the end of the week." The landlord told us.

We paid the deposit and then headed out to explore our city more.

It was an exciting time in life.

Chapter Four: July 1967

We got moved in and immediately started making the place our own. It felt like a dream that I never wanted to wake up from or like we were playing house.

Yet, I felt so grown up in an apartment, paying bills and cleaning, making love all with my best friend. I'd just need to get a job to complete my transition to this chapter.

Since the apartment was so small, we had to be creative with decorating, but there were plenty of secondhand stores nearby, making it easy to find just what we needed.

First, we bought a couch and a bed with some money our parents had given us. Then, a neighbor was moving out and offered us their kitchen table. It was a bit wobbly, but it came with two chairs, and that's all we needed.

With those essential pieces in place, I hit more thrift stores for funky knick-knacks that would turn this little box into our home and kill time while Walter worked. It was fun to put my style into our home and make it feel like ours.

He worked roughly nine hours a day and would come home exhausted. I tried to have dinner on the table when he walked in or soon after. It was the least I could do while I was still not working.

But I quickly got bored with being home, and once the house was settled, it was time for me to start my job search. The only problem was, I wasn't sure exactly how to find a job, as I'd never worked before.

I'd go through the newspaper each day and circle what I thought might fit. Then I'd go to the office only to be turned away for lack of experience. But despite all the rejection, I was hopeful that something would come along. I was either amazingly naïve or ridiculously optimistic. Either way, I knew my opportunity was out there somewhere. I just needed someone to give me a chance.

Today I was wearing my new maroon tweed skirt suit that I'd found at a thrift shop. I slid the list of employers in my pocketbook and then headed out.

"Hello, I'm here about the switchboard job," I said, at the first place.

"Have you run a switchboard before?"

"No, but I'm a fast learner."

"Yes, well, that may be so, but you must have experience." She scoffed, "Thank you for stopping by."

This was the answer I had been getting all week, but how was I supposed to get experience without first having a job?

The places didn't require experience wanted at least some training or college. Without experience and having no college, I wasn't sure what I would do.

I was younger than most of the other women I saw applying and those working in the offices. But I knew I could do the work if someone would just take a chance.

It was nearing lunch, and I was feeling discouraged, so I stumbled into a diner for a cup of coffee and a sandwich. I took a seat in the corner, away from most of the other patrons.

I was feeling homesick and frustrated. This adventure was not turning out how I thought it would. Tears slowly and quietly fell from my eyes.

"What's wrong, young lady?" A strange man asked as he took a seat next to me and handed me a paper napkin.

"I'm sorry. I thought I was ... well, I thought I was alone here." I offered a weak smile as I took the napkin and dabbed my eyes.

"I'm sorry to intrude. You just looked like you needed a friend."

I finally looked up at the man. He was an older gentleman, maybe late 50s, with salt and pepper, thinning hair, kind blue eyes, and a friendly smile.

"Thanks. I'm just having one of those days."

"Tell me about it." His friendly tone was comforting.

I sighed, "I've just moved here with my boyfriend, and I'm having a terrible time finding a job."

"What type of work do you do?"

"Hmm, honestly," I blushed, "I haven't really had a job before. Just babysitting. Everyone is looking for experience or a degree, neither of which I have."

"Yes, that can be tough."

"Yes, but I can type. I've been typing most of my life."

"Oh yeah, how fast are you?"

"80 words per minute."

"Impressive. What else?"

"I worked on my school's newspaper. I wrote two weekly columns for it. One was about the sports teams, and the other was more of an opinion piece about current events."

"No kidding. That's experience." He smiled.

"It is?"

"Absolutely. Have you ever done any filing?"

"Not really, but how hard could it be. I learned the alphabet as a toddler."

He laughed, "Well, I have an idea. Why don't you come to work for me? I have a couple of openings for typists. If you are as good as you say, I'm sure you will move up the company in no time."

"Really?"

"Yes." He slid a card my way.

The name on the card was Eugene Butler, Groove Fashions

"You work at Groove Fashions?"

"I own it."

My mouth dropped open. Here I was, spilling my guts to the owner of my favorite magazine. I took a deep breath to compose myself.

"I would love to work there."

"Great." He dropped a couple of bills on the counter, signaled the waitress, "Follow me. We can go get everything rolling now so you can start tomorrow."

I hesitated only a moment because this couldn't be real. But he had a business card and a warm face, so for that reason, I trusted he wasn't luring me to a dark alley to kill me.

He chatted away on the walk to his office, but I don't know if I replied or if I did; it was automatic responses. I was too awestruck.

"I think you will fit right in with the other girls." He said, "The work is pretty easy if you are used to typing, which it sounds like you are."

I nodded.

"We print once a month, so everything has to be ready by then, so things get chaotic leading up to that. Otherwise, you work mostly at your own pace."

It was on the tip of my tongue to ask how he started the magazine and what his inspirations were, but we soon arrived at a tall beige building.

We stepped inside to a spacious lobby buzzing with activity. People in suits coming and going, chatting back and forth. Behind the reception area sat the elevator banks. As we walked towards the elevators, he was greeted by everyone who walked by.

Inside the elevator, he pushed the button for the twentieth floor. When the elevator lurched to life, taking us up, my stomach did a little somersault.

We finally arrived at the floor, and I was greeted by more hustle and bustle, though a different vibe than in the lobby. We walked down the hall towards an office.

"Knock, knock. Jan?" He said.

A woman in a purple plaid suit and a stylish beehive hairdo looked up from her desk with a smile.

"Hello, Mr. Butler. Who do you have here?" She asked, turning her smile towards me.

"This is Caroline. I've just hired her to take one of the typist jobs."

"Well, that's wonderful and makes my job easier." She chuckled, "I will take care of the paperwork."

"Here, Caroline, have a seat." He motioned for me to sit, "Jan, just bring her back to me when you are done, please."

"Of course." She smiled at me, "Here, let me grab you an application."

She pulled open a drawer in her desk, thumbed through a file, and then handed me the application and a pen. I got right to work filling it out.

"So, how did you meet Mr. Butler?" She asked.

"Oh, hm," I hesitated because it was a too-good-to-be-true story. Who would believe it? "I was over at a diner having lunch, and we got to talking."

"That's so him. He is such a nice man. His wife is even sweeter." She laughed lightly, "You'll meet her soon. She's always here."

"Nice," I smiled, "What's it like here?"

"Fast-paced, but fun." She said, "I love coming to work. I used to work at another company, and it was awful. Now don't get me wrong, like any place, it has its issues, and things can get ... tense, but Mr. Butler is fair and treats everyone here well."

We continued our small talk while I completed my application. It didn't take me long as I didn't have much experience, but thanks to Mr. Butler, I added my time working on the school newspaper and my typing speed.

When I was done, I handed it over to her. She quickly skimmed.

"Great. This looks good." She stood, "I'll take you to Mr. Butler now."

As we walked through the open area where she said I'd be working, she introduced me to a few people. Everyone was smiling and seemed happy. A stark contrast to the offices I had seen this week, though I'd only gotten a peek. Those at their desks seemed to be head's down busy working.

"Is it always like this?" I asked her.

"Yes, I told you. This is a great place to work. You got lucky to have met him." She winked, "Here we are."

She knocked on the open door.

"Oh, Caroline, come in. Thanks, Jan." He said, setting down some pictures, "I was just going through our next edition. So, what do you think of the office so far?"

"It seems wonderful. I can't thank you enough for this opportunity."

"Don't let me down." He said with a chuckle and a wink. "Now, salary. I pay $80 a week, and again, I'm sure you will quickly move up within the company. I have a good feeling about you."

"I ... thank you so much."

"My pleasure. I think you will be a great addition to our team." He said and then stood, "Well, let me walk you out, and we'll see you back here at 8 am tomorrow, yes?"

"Yes."

Leaving, I had to find the bus stop and determine which route would get me home. It looked like I would have to take one bus and then walk a block over to catch a second one. The second one would stop two blocks from our apartment. That should work.

As I made my way to the first bus stop, I couldn't stop smiling. I took in all the sights and landmarks. But I also tried not to daydream too much as I needed to remember how to find the building alone tomorrow.

At least, Jan had given me the address on a slip of paper too, so worst case, if I got lost, I could ask for directions.

I found the first bus easily and got to the second stop just in time to see the bus pulling away. So I'd have to wait for the next one. I hope it didn't take long, as I wanted to stop by the store to grab something special for dinner.

My plan was to make Walt's favorite of pan-fried pork chops with peas and mashed potatoes. I smiled, thinking about him now. I couldn't wait to tell him my news.

I checked my watch, tapping my toe with impatience as I waited.

"It should be here any moment, miss." A gentleman in a double-breasted blue suit said.

"Oh, thanks."

It finally arrived, and soon I was bouncing my way along. I was thankful for the movement of the bus. The anticipation of telling Walter my news had me squirming in my seat. In fact, I wanted to yell out loud to the world.

At my stop, I turned towards the grocery store one block up and two blocks west. I picked up all the items I needed and quickly headed home.

I got right to work, and before long, the entire meal was complete. I set the table and then went to freshen up. When he got home, I wanted to have everything perfect, and I only had minutes to spare.

At exactly 6:00 pm, in walks my love. He looked tired, but his smile filled the room when he saw me.

"There's my girl." He pulled me in for a kiss, "It smells wonderful in here, and don't you look gorgeous."

He pulled me out to take a better look at me and then kissed me once more.

I giggled, "I made pan-fried pork chops and gravy with all your favorites."

"Wow, how'd I get so lucky?"

We sat at the table. After we said our prayer, he dug right in. It made all my hard work worth it to see him enjoying the meal, and maybe that made me sound old-fashioned, but I didn't care.

"This is excellent, Caroline." He said between bites, "So how was your day?"

"Well, it was pretty rotten. I went to all those places on my list. Nobody would give me a shot."

"I'm sorry. I'm sure something will turn up. We still have a little nest egg plus my job, so we'll be fine." He smiled. That single dimple made me swoon a bit.

"Actually, I got a job."

"You did? Oh, that's great. Where?"

"Groove Fashions. I'll be working as a typist."

"That's amazing. We should go out and celebrate."

I giggled, "Yes, but not too late; I have work tomorrow."

We finished our dinner, got things cleaned up together, and then headed out on the town.

Chapter Five: July 1967 - New Job

The next day, I started my job. I was wearing one of my new suits. They weren't actually new, I had found them at a secondhand shop, but they were in near perfect condition at a fraction of the cost.

This one was a charcoal gray with a round collar and a straight skirt. I added the broach a great-aunt had given me for graduation, then with my best heels and slim handbag, I was ready to go.

Walt had to leave a few hours before me, so he didn't get to see me dressed for my first day.

"I hope you have a great first day and that you take over."

"Yeah, wouldn't that be something?" I laughed.

As I made my way through the crowded street, along with the others heading to work, I imagined what my day might be like. Working at a fashion magazine had to be so glamorous.

Would I get to draft my own articles and design my own column showing my love of fashion? Would I work with models and hobnob with designers? Maybe not on the first day, but perhaps one day.

I stifled a giggle as I boarded my first bus. I watched out the window as the city blurred, taking me to my job. I arrived at the office with only minutes to spare. Jan met me at the reception area downstairs and then showed me to my assigned desk.

"Here's your desk. Paper is in the drawer here. Extra ribbon is kept in the supply cabinet down the hall. Restroom is down that hall to your left. Lunch is at noon. You get thirty minutes." She handed me a stack of papers with all kinds of marks on them, "Here are your first assignments for the day. Any questions?"

I looked around at the other ladies. They were either typing away or getting settled with their documents. Unlike yesterday, nobody was talking or laughing. They were all just focused on the task at hand.

"Just one? What do I do with these?"

"Retype this with the corrections. When you finish a page, it goes in this bin here." She pointed to a black file box on one corner of my desk, "Marty will come around to collect throughout the day. New work will go into this one." She pointed to a gun-metal gray box on the opposite side of the desk. "Clock out for the day at 5 sharp."

"Alright. Thank you." I placed my purse in the small drawer in the desk and then sat in the hard, plastic chair. I looked at the girl closest to me. She had a small stack of the pages on a document holder, and the rest were in the gray box. So I copied her setup, adding just a few pages to the holder, and the rest went into the box.

"Be sure you keep them in order." She whispered to me, "They will come by and add pages throughout the day, and if they get out of order... well, Mr. Butler is nice, but not the Editors."

"Oh, okay." I quickly looked at the documents. How could I keep them in order? I could barely read them with all the chicken scratch on them.

She looked around and then came over.

"Here, let me show you."

She quickly gave me a tutorial on the system. The marks were proofreading marks, and they all meant something different. If they wanted to remove a word, the word got a mark through it that looked like a pig's tail. A snake on its side meant to reverse the words. Three lines under a letter meant capitalize it.

It all made sense, but when I was in school writing for the newspaper, I edited my own work and used my own style of marks. I'd never learned this way before.

"And this is how you can tell if the articles and stories go together, see the headings and numbers?"

I nodded. This wasn't what I thought I would be doing, but it wasn't that difficult, especially after she explained it.

"I hope that helps." She looked around, "We aren't really supposed to talk much, but if you get stuck, let me know. I'm Diane."

"Thanks. I'm Caroline."

With that, we both got to work. By lunchtime, I had the system down pretty well. I had gotten through the first stack, and as promised, more came to us throughout the morning.

"Want to join us for lunch, Caroline?" Diane asked as she grabbed her bag, waving to a few of the girls to wait up.

"Oh, yes, I'd love that." I grabbed my bag and followed them.

We all packed into the elevator, everyone chatting and giggling as the elevator took us down to the bottom floor, where there was a cafeteria.

"If you give them your name and what floor you work on, they will just take it out of your check each week," Diane informed me as we got in the line for lunch.

I followed Diane closely, so I didn't mess up. She grabbed a tray and silverware, so did I. She placed her order when she got to the item she wanted, and so did I. I ordered a half sandwich with soup. Then we went over to a drink station and then to a cashier.

"Caroline Graham. Twentieth floor." I said.

"She works with me, Hazel," Diane said.

"Great. Got ya."

With payment taken care of, I followed the rest of the typist from my floor to a table.

Diane made quick introductions. There were five others besides us, and I knew it would take me a day or two to remember everyone's names, especially if we didn't get to speak much.

I listened and ate while the others gossiped and chatted like long-time friends. They were all a few years older than me, which made me feel even more out of place, but I was still excited to be included and working to help Walt.

"So, Caroline, what's your story?" one of the girls asked. I think her name was Betty.

"Oh, me? My boyfriend and I just moved here from Virginia. We are working towards getting married in the future and starting a family."

I mentally chastised myself for my overshare. I could have just said we'd just moved here and left it at that.

"Probably have big dreams, huh?" She laughed, "I was like you once. Unfortunately, this town will squash those right out of you."

"Betty, that's rude." Diane said, then offered me a weak smile, "Don't listen to her. She's just bitter because her man just left her for another woman."

"Hey, don't tell her all my business." Betty pouted.

"Then don't be rude."

"I think it's sweet. That's how I got here too. Followed a man." Another girl said. I couldn't remember her name. Marley, maybe? Mary? Marianne? I'd get it down.

I smiled at her and twirled the spoon around in the last of my soup. I didn't know how to respond to her. Were they trying to tell me

Walter would leave me? I couldn't and wouldn't believe it. He loved me.

"Oh, we better hustle up. Lunch is almost over." Diane said, looking at the clock.

We all grabbed our trays and made our way to a conveyor belt, setting the trays down. Then, they were magically carried off to the kitchen or who knows where?

Back in the elevator, the mood was not as festive as it had been at the start of our break and got gloomier the higher up we went. A quick trip to the lady's room, and then we were all back in front of our typewriters pounding away.

Before I knew it, the day was over, and it was time to head home. It would take me roughly thirty minutes to get there, so dinner for Walt and I would have to be something easy.

I arrived home to find that he was already home and trying his best to cook for me.

"Walt, what are you doing home already?"

"I asked to leave a bit early so I could come home and make you dinner." He grinned, "Being your first day, I wanted to surprise you."

"Oh, my, that is the sweetest thing." I couldn't imagine my dad ever cooking for my mom. "Do you know how to cook?"

He gave a sheepish grin, "Honestly, no, but how hard could it be?"

I joined him in the kitchen to see he was trying to brown some ground meat and had what looked like pasta in water, but it was ice cold still. There was a jar of sauce on the counter.

"Spaghetti?"

"Yes, I know it's your favorite, but the pasta is just a rock." He stirred it with a spoon, and it all moved together, "I'm not sure when the meat is done." He then jabbed it with the spoon.

"Here, let me help." I cranked up the heat under the meat and then scooped all the pasta out and just started that over. While the water heated up, I grabbed some lettuce and tomatoes, making us a quick salad. Then took a few slices of bread out, slathered it with butter, and placed it in the toaster oven.

With the water boiling, I dumped in a new box of pasta and then drained the fat off the meat before adding the tomato sauce. I then pulled out a variety of my favorite spices and added them to the sauce, tasting as I did.

Walter stood by, drinking a beer and watching in awe, "It's amazing, Caroline. You make it look so easy."

"I love doing this for you, so that makes it easy." Honestly, I'd been cooking most of my life, and I loved it.

"I don't think I need to tell you, but I've never cooked before. Well, nothing more than some eggs and toast."

"Yeah, I could tell." I giggled and leaned forward to kiss him.

"So, tell me, how did your first day go?"

We talked while the food finished cooking, and then we sat at our small two-person table. He had set the table beautifully for us with our best set of plates.

I'd gotten them at a thrift store for next to nothing. They were beige with sunflowers on them. Looking at them made me smile. They were happy plates.

"It sounds like you had a good day."

"I did. I was a little nervous at the start, but it got easier. It helped that I had a helpful neighbor."

After dinner, he made me go sit while he washed up. I knew I'd likely have to go behind him, but bless his heart, he tried, and I loved that.

I flipped on our little television. All the channels playing the news at the moment. It was full of images from Vietnam.

While the news played, I picked up a magazine from the side table and flipped through it. I loved all the new outfits, but I also studied the structure and the layout of each page.

"What if I change my hair up a bit?" I asked.

"I love you as you are, but if that would make you happy, I would love it." He said, drying his hands and then joining me on the sofa. I stretched my legs out across his lap. He began rubbing them gently.

"Aw, you are always so sweet to me."

We snuggled together on the couch. Having gone out nearly every night, it was nice to spend one night at home.

As we watched television, I thought about my first day in the workforce. It had been incredible. While the work was entry-level, I think I would enjoy it a lot.

I also wanted to learn all I could as fast as possible, so I could hopefully move up to a junior copy editor and then editor one day. It was my dream to write.

Thinking about work reminded me of what the other girls had said at lunch.

"Walt, you won't ever leave me, right?"

"Of course not. Why would you ask that?"

"Oh, no reason."

I knew in my heart that he wouldn't leave me, but I had let the gossip at lunch get to me. He loved me, and I knew that would never change.

Chapter Six: March 1968

Our life had a nice routine to it. We both went to work each day then I would race home each evening to cook for us, which I loved doing.

Some nights we would go out to nightclubs or bars. Sometimes we'd go out with friends, other nights we stayed just the two of us.

My favorite routine was Sunday morning before church. He'd run down to the corner to grab the morning newspaper. I'd make us breakfast and coffee. Then we'd read the paper together while eating.

It was the best hour of the week.

However, one day, I came home with an armful of groceries to find Walt pacing the floor.

"Walt, you're home early. What's wrong?"

He took a deep breath, "I was fired today."

"Fired? For what?" I sat as the room spun a little.

"They said they had too many men in the mailroom and the last in, first out."

"Oh, that's awful. What are you going to do? What are we going to do?"

"Well, that's what I want to talk to you about." He took my hands and pulled me towards our table, "I talked to an Army recruiter today."

"You did what? To join that war?" I felt tears well in my eyes.

"Yes, yes. I think it is the right choice for me, for us. I'll get paid, and we will have some benefits."

"But you will have to go to war." The images played in my mind. I didn't know anyone personally that had been killed, and hopefully never would, but I had heard stories. "I thought you wouldn't leave me."

"I'm not, well not forever." He took my hands, "It will be temporary, and I'll be back before you know it."

"I can't ... you can't."

"Do you trust me?"

"I do but what does that have to do with this?"

"Do you trust that when I say I will come back, that I will?"

I thought about his words for a moment. I knew the risk; how could he promise me something like that?

We talked about it for hours, and hours turned into days until finally I gave in and agreed to him joining. I cried quietly each night after he was asleep.

Days before he was leaving, he came to me with a proposal. Not the type of proposal I had expected, but more of a business one. I wanted romance and to be caught off guard.

"Caroline, we should marry before I leave."

I laughed, thinking he was joking, "Oh, Walt, you're funny."

"No, I'm serious. I want to make sure that you would get any money and benefits I have if I don't, you know, make it back."

"I can't even think like that." I said with a huff, "I know you will come back. You said I could trust you not to leave me. Plus, unfinished business will give you the will to live. What a good story that would make!"

"Of course, I'll come back, but we need to have a serious talk about this. If something happens to me, and even if it doesn't, you will get benefits." He frowned, "I think it would be worth our while to do it before I leave."

"No, I just won't. I feel like it is almost a jinx to marry you now. I believe completely that you will be killed if we marry, but you will make it back to me if we wait. You will have to so you can keep your promise to me. It is the only hope I have."

"Your naivety is one of those things I love about you, but I'm worried that this time you're not being smart," He sighed, "But I can't force you. I can only tell you how I feel and why. You have to make the decision."

"If all goes well, you shouldn't be gone that long, and then we can get married. I just know everything will be okay."

And I know I was being childish and silly about all of this, but I just couldn't jinx us.

He scooped me up into his lap, kissing me softly and holding me tight. But we didn't talk about it again. I almost wish he would have pushed the issue more or asked me again. But, my resolve was weak, and I would have given in.

But we were still young, and I just felt there was plenty of time left. The years ahead of us were more than the years behind. Plus, he said he would never leave me, so this separation would be temporary.

The last night we spent together, the night before he left for boot camp, we slept very little. I spent the night memorizing his face, his hands, his chest, just all of him. I had to have something to remember to get me through the next year or possibly two.

I tried to stop time and keep the morning from coming, but my will wasn't strong enough. Finally, before either of us was ready, it was time for him to leave. I cried and begged him not to leave, to tell them he'd changed his mind, but it was no use. He had to go.

He kissed me and walked away. I know he had to, but my heart broke into a million pieces, but I had to hold on to the hope he would be back. He'd promised.

I spent the whole day in bed crying, begging the universe to send him back. It was pointless, I know, but I didn't know how I would live without him. It was different than just being separated during the workday. This was for who knows how long.

Maybe he would be one of the lucky ones that he didn't have to go to Vietnam. He could get stationed somewhere else, maybe even somewhere in the United States, like Georgia or Texas. I had heard of several people that hadn't gone to Vietnam. If that was the case, maybe I would join him, and we could get married then.

I continued sobbing until I had nothing left to give, collapsing into the sofa; emotionally exhausted, I slept.

Somehow, I got up the next day to go to work. I adored my job and most of the people I worked with, so throwing myself into work would be a good distraction. Plus, the apartment felt so empty without him.

We were in crunch week, which meant all the articles had to be finalized for print by the end of the week. We were always rushed, but right before printing, it got crazier.

It also meant any time off had to be approved by Mr. Butler as they didn't usually let anyone off. However, after I explained why, he understood my request and needed to take off yesterday.

"My own son is in the Army, so I completely understand. Take as much time as you need." He had said.

When I arrived, I immediately got down to work. Grabbing the first story in my stack and began typing out the corrected article. I kept my head down as much as possible. I wanted to avoid people today, and the less eye contact I made, the better.

"Hi, Caroline." Though we didn't normally socialize during the day, she couldn't help herself.

"Oh, hi, Betty." I tried to keep working, but it kind of breaks your focus when you had the biggest gossip at your desk.

"I noticed you weren't in yesterday. I'm surprised that you were allowed to take off since it *is* crunch week. Were you sick?"

The expression on her face made me want to punch her right in the teeth, and I'm not a violent person. I don't even like to kill flies. Instead, I shoo them out the window, but Betty brought out the worst in me.

"I just had some ... personal business. It was approved by Mr. Butler."

I wanted to add more, but I just held my tongue and kept my eyes scanning the current page I was reviewing, but my hands didn't move across the typewriter. I didn't see any of the words, but maybe she would take the hint if I looked busy.

"Well, I heard it was because your boyfriend is off to boot camp. Is that true?"

"Hm, yes."

"Well, why do you get special treatment when the rest of us can't take off during crunch week?" She huffed.

"*That*, Betty, is none of your business. I approved her to be out, and that's all you need to know." Thank the good Lord for Mr. Butler, "Now, I am *sure* you have deadlines to meet, yes?" His tone was clear and to the point.

"Yes, sir." She glared at me from behind his back as she walked away.

By lunch, I'm sure it would be spread that I was Mr. Butler's favorite or worse, that we were having an affair. Though anyone with half a brain knew he wouldn't ever cheat on his wife. He was a good man and acted more like a father figure. Not like the Editors who would have had our heads had one of them caught us chatting like that.

"Thank you, Mr. Butler. I appreciate that."

"You're welcome. I just wanted to check to see how you were holding up today."

"I'm... fine." But, unfortunately, I wasn't, and my voice clearly gave me away.

"I know, Caroline. If it wasn't crunch week, I would have insisted you take another day or two off, at least but unfortunately, I can't spare a single person, especially not my fastest, most accurate typist."

"Thanks." That made my day a little brighter.

He smiled then walked away. I got back to work, and his compliment boosted my motivation.

"Wow, Caroline," Marty said as he dropped off more work for me an hour later, "You're flying through your stacks."

"Thanks. I'm trying."

"Do you want me to leave more for you?"

I eyed the inbox and knew I could get through that in less than an hour.

"Yes, you can leave me a few extras."

"Alright." He thumbed through to ensure he had complete articles and dropped them in the box with a smile.

There was a deep sigh from behind me. I knew the tone well. Betty clearly disgusted by my ability. I didn't care and ignored her attitude.

The rest of the day was uneventful unless you count Betty sneering at me each time she walked by or sighing anytime someone else spoke to me.

Was it my imagination, or was she walking by an unusual amount of times today? We rarely got up from our machines, but she must have found every excuse in the book to get up.

I took my time heading back to the apartment. I just couldn't bear the thought of eating without him. Cooking for him had been one of my favorite parts of the day. He would always rave about whatever meal I had made for him. I smiled, thinking about it as a lone tear slid quietly down my face.

Instead of cooking, I bought myself a tv dinner. It was the turkey version. I thought it would remind me of Thanksgiving and cheer me up. It didn't, but at least the clean-up was easy as I put most of it in the trash.

After I'd finished my meal, I didn't know what to do with myself. I knew I wasn't going to go out alone and I needed to avoid the television because at this time of the evening it would be nothing but news. I couldn't handle seeing anything about that war.

Instead, I pulled out my stationery kit and started writing letters. One to my mother, one to my childhood friend, Dottie, and another to Walter. The recruiter had given us an address we could send him letters to but said it would take a while to get to him.

With nothing left to distract me, I watched the TV until I fell asleep on the sofa. When the station went off the air for the night, it woke me. I stared at it for a moment, confused from being woken up. I then sat up slightly to switch off the television before rolling over falling back asleep.

So ended my first day alone.

Chapter Seven: May 1968

After a little over a month on my own, my mother was coming to keep me company. The plan was for her to stay for a week or two as her schedule was flexible. It would be a nice distraction from thinking about Walter and how lonely I was here without him.

Though I had made a few friends, it wasn't the same. They were casual friends, not ones I spent a lot of time with. Walt was my person. We had a special connection, or at least I had always thought so.

I missed our routine, especially those Sunday mornings with breakfast and the paper. I missed sitting on the couch in the evening, catching up on our day, or getting dressed up to meet friends at a bar or watch a movie.

My current routine was quite depressing. I worked all day and then spent most of the night crying into my pillow with the television for my only company. TV dinners had become my go-to meal, though sometimes I grabbed a sandwich or soup from the deli down the street.

Some of the girls at work had invited me out with them a few times. I went a hand full of time, but the dancing and music just reminded me of Walter, and I most of the time, I left early.

Over time, they simply stopped asking, and honestly, that was fine with me. Had they asked, I would have turned them down.

With my mother's impending visit, it gave me a nice distraction as I spent my entire weekend cleaning the apartment from top to bottom.

After ensuring the bedsheets were cleaned and pressed, I made up my bed for her as I planned to sleep on the sofa. I slept there now most nights anyway, so it wouldn't be a significant change from how I'd been living.

I scrubbed the floors, the counters, and everything in between. The whole place gleamed when I was done. I felt good and also exhausted.

She would arrive today after I was home from work. My dad was driving her, and he would stay the night before going home. I couldn't wait to see them.

I rushed home to freshen up a bit before they arrived, plus I didn't want them waiting on the street until I got there. But, of course, today my first bus was late in picking us up, so then I missed the second one. It was a nearly everyday occurrence, but couldn't today of all days, the stars align.

When I finally got off at my stop, I was 15 minutes later getting home than I wanted, and as I came around the corner to my block, there they were leaning against the metallic blue Impala in their traveling clothes. My mother was fanning herself while my dad finished a cigarette and checked his watch.

I felt hot tears form at the sight and rushed the remaining steps to them. I'd known I was homesick, but seeing them, I wanted nothing more than that feeling of security that only your family could bring.

"I'm sorry I'm late. You're a little earlier than I expected, though." I said as I rushed into my mother's arms.

"Caroline, you look so wonderful." My mother said. She produced a couple of tissues, handing me one as she dabbed at her own eyes.

"We made excellent time." My dad bragged. "Almost no traffic, and the gas mileage on the freeway was excellent."

"Well, why don't we go in so you can freshen up and get settled before dinner." I offered.

My father grabbed the bags, and they followed me upstairs. I was so proud of my little home and couldn't wait for them to see it.

"Oh, this is wonderful, Caroline." My mother said as we stepped inside, "You have really made a nice home here."

I tried to look around my house through their eyes, taking in all my resale finds. Would the mustard and brown couch with the dark red and green pillows and my favorite blanket draped over the back look like someone's ugly discard instead of my favorite place to sit? Would the various knick-knacks on shelves by the one window be tacky and childish? The window also held a couple of potted plants in funky painted pots. Would they understand how adorable I thought they were?

In the kitchen nook, I had a mint green Formica topped table with four matching chairs. It was an upgrade from the hand-me-down from our neighbors. I had found this one at a sidewalk sale a few months ago.

The rest of my kitchen was simple with just the bare necessities. I'd worked hard to get all the grime from the former tenants cleaned up, and I'd like to think it showed.

"You can put the bags in my bedroom this way." I pointed my father to the room. "The bathroom is here."

He set the bags down while my mom hurried into the bathroom. I got them each a drink and brought them to the coffee table. We visited for a bit before heading to dinner. They both changed from their traveling clothes to supper attire.

I decided that my navy-blue shift dress with the white peter pan collar and cuffs that I'd worn to work would be perfect for the steakhouse we were going to, so I didn't change, but I did redo my hair and make-up for a more evening look and added a white wool jacket and a pillbox hat.

The steakhouse was far enough that we would have to drive. We opted to take a taxi, which was much easier than having my father drive. We arrived just a few minutes before our reservation and had a short wait before being seated.

I hadn't been here yet but had heard good things from some of the girls at work. Diane had come on a date once.

"Get the porterhouse. It is the most!" She had told me when I mentioned my parents' visit.

We got seated, and the waiter greeted us, letting us know the specials and taking our drink order. He then left us to browse the menu.

"My friend recommended the porterhouse, in case you want an idea." I offered.

"Mm, alright. I think that's what I'm getting." My dad mumbled.

My mom decided on the lamb chops. We also ordered creamed spinach and Lyonnaise potatoes. The waiter brought us a basket of fresh, hot rolls and creamy butter, and we each got a fresh garden salad topped with homemade croutons and house dressing.

The steak was cooked to a perfect medium and melted in your mouth. The potatoes were garlicky and had the right balance of onion and butter flavor.

My mother and I made small talk as we ate, while my father focused solely on his meal. He had always been a man of few words and only spoke when necessary.

"And I can't remember if I told you that Larry and Mary Jane are having a baby?"

"No, really?" This would be a first grandchildren for my parents and a niece or nephew for me. Larry was the oldest, and then I had two other brothers, Karl and Dean. Neither of them was married yet, though I suspected Karl was close. Being the only girl and several years younger, I seldom talked to them, "When is the baby due?"

"Early October." She smiled, "It's exciting. We'll be grandparents."

She touched my dad's hand. He looked at her for only a moment, but you could see the love in their gaze. Something I wanted in my future marriage. They had always been a wonderful example for us kids.

"So, after dinner, I thought we could go to Time Square or maybe a carriage ride in Central Park?"

"A carriage ride would be fun." My mom said.

My father's ordinarily stoic expression fell flat, telling me that he didn't think it would be fun. I looked away from him so as not to laugh out loud.

"Great. I know just where to go." I said.

Walter and I had taken a carriage ride once when we first moved here. It had been a beautiful night for it, and we got to take in some of the sights.

I glanced at my mother. She would love everything except the smell. My father would simply be happy that she enjoyed herself, but he would likely hate every minute of it.

So once the meal was eaten, doggy bags put together, and the bill taken care of, we hailed a cab and asked to take us to the sixth avenue entrance north of Central Park South. I knew that they would have carriages lined up just waiting for tourists to rent them for a ride.

I pointed out some of the landmarks on our drive over. My mother was so excited about everything and asked a million questions. I couldn't answer them all but thank goodness for the driver. He knew everything.

"Yeah, so Time Square is a block that way. You got the Empire State buildin' this-a-way, and the Hudson River is that-a-way." He pointed.

"I can't wait to see everything." My mom said lightly, clapping her hands.

My father didn't say a word; he merely slipped his hand into my mother's and smiled at her. She smiled back. I instantly felt like a third wheel but happy that my parents were still in love after all these years.

We got to the park and found an available carriage. We climbed in, and then the driver guided the horse around the park. My mother giggled like a schoolgirl as she settled into the seat.

I couldn't enjoy the ride as much as I'd hoped. My heart ached for Walter as I remembered the last time we were here together. It had been so romantic, even with the strong horse manure smell.

I had yet to hear from him and was worried. How was he doing with basic training? Was he eating well? He was quite fit from his days playing sports, so I wasn't concerned about him keeping up physically. It was just everything else about it. He had such a kind spirit, and I didn't want that to change.

The ride came to an end, and we walked the few blocks to my apartment. My parents walked hand-in-hand with me leading the way.

Once back at my apartment, we took turns in the bathroom, and then my parents settled into my bedroom for the night. I got comfortable on the sofa, so thankful my parents were here, which meant I wasn't alone.

For the first night in a long time, I didn't cry myself to sleep.

Chapter Eight: September 1968

Finally, today was the day Walter came home for his 30 days leave before heading to his assignment. But, unfortunately, we hadn't gotten lucky, and his orders would be taking him to Vietnam.

But, for today, he would be here with me. I waited impatiently at the airport for my love to arrive. We would spend time part of his visit here in New York, just the two of us, and then part of it back home with our families.

His flight was arriving in the late evening, so thankfully, I didn't have to take off work. As it was, I would be taking off a week to go back to Virginia and hated to ask for more. I always had guilt about taking time off. Maybe it was Betty and her attitude towards me. Or perhaps the fact that I loved my job and most everyone else I worked with. Whatever the reason, I hated to be away too long.

My stomach fluttered a bit as I waited. It was crowded. I looked around at the other anxious faces. Everyone

I smoothed the front of my new dress. It was a mustard yellow empire dress with large white polka dots that my mother had sewed for me during her visit.

She was always one to find a pattern and sewing machine. While I was at work one day during her visit, she made friends with one of my older neighbors. They had a sewing party, and so my new dress was born, along with a few other creations.

His flight finally arrived. I watched it taxi, and they pushed a stairwell out to the plane. Then after several minutes, the passenger began to deplane.

My pulse quickened. Soon I'd see him. My lover, my best friend.

Suddenly, he was walking towards me. He looked dashing in his uniform, but I didn't like the military-style haircut. He had beautiful, thick dark hair, and at current, it was so short that you almost couldn't tell its color or how it has a slight wave to it when damp.

"Caroline!" He said, scooping me up.

The tears began as soon as he touched me. We held each other.

That's when the yelling started from all around us. Strangers interrupted our happy moment. People that just minutes before, I thought were waiting to welcome loved ones were here to protest them.

"Baby killer!"

"Murderer!"

"Peace not war!"

I was so confused. It was more than those who had been waiting here, but where had they all come from? And, why here? Why during our moment?

I knew that people were protesting and angry, but this was Walter. My sweet, thoughtful boyfriend. He wasn't a baby killer or a murderer.

"Come on, Caroline, let's get out of here." He took my hand, and we hurried away, but the small mob followed us. "They told us a bit about this. Best not to engage at all."

We made our way to baggage claim to wait for his bag. The protesters were relentless. Some started throwing trash at us.

"Why are you doing this to us?" I yelled, "You don't know us."

"He kills babies and murder innocents, just like all those over there." One lady yelled back.

"He is a sweet person and would never kill someone like that." I pleaded.

It didn't stop them. They continued to yell insults and slurs at us, well him. Thankfully his bag arrived so we could escape this harassment.

Hailing a cab became another eye-opening experience. Most refused to take us. We finally found someone who would stop and let us in.

"Thank you, sir," Walt said.

"No problem, son. I'm a veteran myself. Fought in World War II."

We gave him the address to our apartment. He smiled and pulled away from the curb.

"It's a real shame how people treatin' you boys. A real shame." The driver said, shaking his head, "My generation was hailed as heroes, and you are seen as worse than the enemy."

"Yeah, I didn't really realize when I enlisted how it would be. I thought it was just a few cells of protesters, but it's not."

They talked through the entire ride while I just held his hand and fought tears. That wasn't fair. I disagreed with the war, but it was simply a job for Walter. A means to provide for his family and to do what our fathers had done. Fight for our country.

And no matter how someone felt about the fight, shouldn't they support the people? They are human beings, our brothers, cousins, and neighbors. They are someone's husband or father.

And I'd heard all the arguments against the U.S. being there, and I didn't have a strong opinion on it. What I did know was my Walt did not deserve that treatment. If only people knew him, the him I know.

We pulled up at our apartment, thanked our driver, and then climbed the stairs to our floor. We stepped in, and he exhaled heavily as he dropped his bags.

"Ah, it feels so good to see this place again. To be home with you." He pulled me to him. "I missed you so much."

We kissed our way to the sofa, and that was as far as we made it. Soon clothes started coming off, and the couple of months we had been apart became a distant memory.

Later, we made our way to bed to continue our reunion.

"How was basic training?" I asked.

"It was ... okay."

"That's it, just, okay?"

"It's not something I want to talk about." He sighed and rolled to look at me. "It was hard. They beat us down and then trained us up the way they wanted us to be."

"Do you regret enlisting?"

"Sometimes, but felt right at the time. Now? I just don't know."

"I'm sorry, but maybe you won't have to stay in long, right?"

"Yeah, as soon as I can get out, I will."

"Well, are you excited to head home?"

"Yes. I miss home. I'm ready to see my parents. I want a burger at Sam's place."

"Yes, and a pile of fries."

We reminisced about home and then talked about our future.

"I want four kids." He said as he traced a finger over my stomach and chest.

"You do?"

"Yeah, you had siblings, but I didn't. I want my children to have built-in friends."

"Well, just because you have multiple kids doesn't mean they will be friends with each other. I'm not close with my brothers at all."

"I guess that's true." He said, "How many children do you want then?"

"Oh, I do want a lot of children. The number doesn't matter too much."

"Yeah, I guess I don't really care how many, just as long as they all have your beautiful green eyes."

"And your one dimple." I leaned forward to kiss it now.

"And your gorgeous smile." He leaned forward to kiss me.

"And your thick black hair."

We laughed as we continued to talk and kiss and talk some more. At some point, we both fell asleep. I hadn't slept that well in months.

Since we had sold our car when we moved here, we took the train home. His father came to pick us up at the station. When we arrived, the two Franks men greeted each other with a hug, a hardy handshake, and the senior Franks rubbed the buzz-cut head of his son. Then, they chuckled and smiled awkwardly for a moment.

"Alrighty, let's get you two home," Mr. Franks said.

The train station was roughly an hour away, but as we pulled into our small-town, I looked out the window. I hadn't realized how much I missed the familiar sights. The one grocery store, people waving as we drove by, all the trees and flowers. It was completely different than New York City.

There was our school. It felt like a million years since we walked those halls. It had only been one for me. Three years since I walked them hand in hand with Walter. I smiled, remembering.

I felt like I had grown up a lot in the past year since graduating. But, on the other hand, I couldn't believe it had only been a year.

I looked at Walter. It was going to be hard to let him go again. I wish he would have never enlisted, but if this past year was an indication, time went faster than expected, and soon he would be back.

We pulled up their long driveway, and his mother came running out.

"There's my soldier boy!" She wrapped him in a big hug the second he was out of the car. Now, this was the kind of welcome he should be receiving.

"Hi, mother."

She then came and hugged me, "Come in, you two."

We headed into the house. It smelled like Sunday dinner when we stepped into the house, even though it was Friday.

"I have you both set up in Walt's old room. Sheets are cleaned and ironed. Fresh towels in the bathroom."

"Here, let me get that bag from you, Caroline." His father said, taking it from me.

"Thanks, mom, dad."

"Thanks, Mr. and Mrs. Franks." I followed Walter to his room.

Mr. Franks set my bag down, "Walt, you know where everything is, so I'll leave you to freshen up before dinner."

We washed up and unpacked our bags, then made the mistake of laying down.

"Ah, I could sleep right now." He said with a yawn.

"Me too."

We stayed there probably a minute too long, but when I heard my parents arrive, we stretched and headed down to greet them.

After saying hello, we all got seated for dinner. Mrs. Franks had made a pot roast, mashed potatoes, and glazed carrots. There were also homemade biscuits with homemade strawberry jam. Yum.

"This is the perfect welcome home meal, mom. Thank you."

"Only the best for my son."

Once dinner was done, we ate my mother's apple pie, we moved to the living room to visit.

The big question everyone kept asking me was if I would continue to live in New York once Walter left again.

"I honestly don't know. I hadn't thought about it." I answered.

The conversation turned to other topics, but I continued to think about the question and what I would do after he left again. I looked around at our parents' faces and my love; it was wonderful to be here with them. It should be a fun week as we spent time with our families and childhood friends.

However, I loved our life in New York City, even without him. I'd made a little home in that tiny apartment. It had special touches that made me happy, and I felt comfortable there.

I especially enjoyed my job. I was learning so much about the business, despite still working in the typing pool. I listened to hallway conversations or saw how the articles were structured, and I understood what the editors liked and didn't like based on the corrections I had to type each day.

I didn't have many friends there, but that was okay with me. I was happy, and I knew it would be lonely without Walter, but the time would go quickly, and then he would be back to continue our life together.

With the decision made, I tuned back into the conversation happening around me. Walt was sharing his experience in training.

"It was difficult, but I feel good about my choice."

"You're carrying on the proud military tradition in our family." His father said, "My father served. I served. Several uncles as well."

"Caroline's family too. Longline of military men." My father boasted.

"Well, I don't know about everyone else, but I cannot bring myself to watch the news anymore." Mrs. Franks said.

"Oh, I can't either, Gloria." My mother added, "So many from our little town there or heading there." She looked at me with a weak smile.

I reached over and took Walt's hand, giving it a light squeeze. He squeezed back, but he kept talking to our fathers.

Later that night, the house was quiet. Walter was asleep and laid there staring at the ceiling. He was the love of my life, and I couldn't imagine him not being with me. He'd already been gone far too long. How could I do this unknown amount of time?

Chapter Nine: October 1968

We'd had a pleasant weeklong visit with our families and childhood friends. We had done everything that we'd planned to do, including going bowling and to the drive-in. We had our favorite meals sitting in our favorite booth at the diner. It had been a wonderful time spent reliving our early years.

Unfortunately, we left just before my new niece was born. My mother called the next day to tell me.

"Larry and Mary Jane had the baby last night."

"Really? How is she doing? How's the baby?"

"They are both wonderful. A little girl. 7 pounds 2 ounces and 19 inches long. They named her Denise Ann."

"Aw, sweet." I said, "I wish she would have been born while I was there. I guess I'll see her at Thanksgiving."

"I'll send you some pictures as soon as I get them developed."

We talked a few more minutes before ending the call. I couldn't wait to see pictures of my niece, and I couldn't wait to start my own family with Walter. I looked over at him. He was sitting on the couch reading.

I crossed the room and climbed into his lap, giving him a kiss.

"What was that for?" He asked as he wrapped his arms around my waist.

"I'm just so happy."

We enjoyed the last few hours together before I had to return to work. He was only here for another week, but I couldn't miss more work right now.

The next day, as I made my way to the office, my body tensed as dread washed over me. I wanted to spend every minute I could with Walter before he left for Vietnam. However, being at work for the next eight to nine hours felt like a waste of time when he was about to be sent into a war zone for an undetermined amount of time.

But we had bills to pay, and his wages from the Army weren't enough to cover them all alone.

My buses were all on time, and the foot traffic seemed lighter than usual, so I arrived a few minutes earlier than expected.

I got right to work on my full inbox, trying to keep my head down, and only briefly looked up at a few of my friends when they came in.

Marty had already picked up my first batch of edited work and had dropped off more when Mr. Butler came to my desk.

"Caroline, could you please join me in my office?"

"Yes, of course." I stood, smoothing my skirt, then followed him.

From the corner of my eye, I saw Betty glaring at me. What did she know that I didn't know? Was I in trouble? Was I getting fired?

"Have a seat?" He said, closing the door behind me, "First of all, how're you doing? I know your boyfriend is home."

"I'm well. Thank you."

"Are you sure? I know how difficult it is and how important a visit home is."

"Oh, yes, Mr. Butler." Where was he going with this? "But I'll see him after work."

"Okay, good then." He smiled, "Well, the reason I asked you in here is that we have a Junior Copy Editor position open working with Bert and Sally." He paused. Was I supposed to say something? I smiled. I guess that was the right reaction because he then continued, "And, we'd like to offer it to you."

"Me?"

"Yes. Do you *not* want it?"

I guess my tone was negative or startled, but I was just caught off guard. I really thought I was getting fired.

"Oh, of course, I do, but I ... thank you."

The door opened, and in walked Bert and Sally. They were two of the magazine's best writers. Their specialty was make-up tips and tricks, or at least those were my favorite. They also wrote about the latest trends and new designers.

"She said yes." Mr. Butler told them.

"Oh, wonderful. You were our first choice." Bert said with a smile.

"You are the fastest typist, and we have seen that you have caught some of our mistakes that others have missed, so it would be great to have those extra eyes of yours," Sally said, offering her hand. I shook it.

"I appreciate you both thinking of me for this. I'm very excited to work with you." I was stunned and didn't know what the correct response was.

"We're excited too. We'll have you starting with us tomorrow. No more typing pool. You'll be sitting outside of our office." Bert said.

"I'll show you," Sally said, gesturing for me to follow her.

I had only briefly seen where they sit as I rarely got up during the day and never went in that direction. The ladies' room was the opposite way, and the kitchen was near the typing area, so there was no reason to go down the writer's hall.

As we walked by the typing area, all eyes were on me. A few ladies smiled as I went by. Diane gave me a silent clap, so I smiled briefly in response.

Though there were others, like Betty, who appeared less than happy. They either had their arms crossed over the chests or rolled their eyes and started whispering to a neighbor.

I squared my shoulders and held my head a bit higher. I wasn't going to be anchored to a typewriter and an inbox all day like them. Instead, I would immediately see the new content and be able to offer suggestions.

"Okay, this is us here. You'll be there, right in front of our office." She nodded for me to look in.

Peeking in, I saw two dark wood desks were pushed together facing each other, making one large table. They were littered with papers, pens, and photos. A giant corkboard covered in story ideas and note cards was on one wall.

"So, you will take what we write up and type it out. This is why we wanted you because we think you'll catch all of our mistakes, and then it might not get kicked back as much. Our last girl wasn't good at catching our mistakes, and we had a lot of things get sent to be retyped." She gestured towards the typing pool. "We would rather it spend less time going around. We get paid a bonus for each story that gets published, so the faster the stories are done, the more we can get in each month."

"We have the same hours, so no reason to change that, but you'll get paid more here. We are offering $130 a week."

I almost fell over. That was $50 more than I was making and would help out a lot. Without Walter's previous income, I considered moving into a cheaper apartment or finding a roommate. Though now that Walt was out of basic training, he would start getting a regular paycheck which would help.

"Thank you so much. I won't let you down."

"We know you won't. You were made for this job." Sally said.

After that was done, I floated back to my workstation for my last day as a typist. I couldn't stop smiling. A few of the girls whispered congratulations.

Betty didn't say anything to me directly, though she whispered a lot to her clique of friends, but not a word to me. It didn't matter to me. I was moving up, and she was stuck in the same position she had been in for two years now. She'd likely have a better chance to advance if she had a better attitude.

At quitting time, I practically ran out to catch my bus. Of course, it was running late, which meant I'd miss my second bus, but at least at the end of all of this would be Walter, and I couldn't wait to share my fantastic news in person.

Finally, I made it to our building. I flew up the stairs to our apartment.

"I got a promotion!" I yelled as I opened the door.

"You what?"

"I got promoted to a junior copy editor." I said, breathless as I tried to catch my breath.

"I don't know exactly what that means, but I'm excited for you." He grabbed me in his arms, giving me a long kiss, "Let's go out to celebrate."

We both got dressed up and headed out on the town. He took me to a wonderful Italian restaurant that we couldn't normally afford and then to our favorite nightclub to dance.

It was perfect, but I had to get up early the next day, so we didn't stay out too late. Though late enough, I would definitely be tired the next day. I didn't care. I was young, in love, and moving up in the world.

All too soon, it was time for Walter to leave. We soaked up as much time together as we could.

He did ask me nearly every day if I would reconsider marrying him before he left, but I stood fast in my superstition. I just wanted to give him a reason to try so very hard to come home to me. We had unfinished business. It was naive, I know, but I had to hold on to some hope.

His parents flew up a few days before to spend some last moments with him. They stayed in a hotel not too far away.

They had a great time being tourists with Walt while I was working my new job. Sally and Bert had been right. It was a perfect fit. The work was more enjoyable, and I often was brought into their brainstorming meetings. I soaked up every bit of information I could about the process. I wanted to move up to their jobs one day.

But for today, I was off, so I could say goodbye, again, to my soul mate, my best friend.

His parents had a flight out about an hour after his. So, once I left the airport, I would be alone.

Again, he was heckled by a crowd of protestors. It was an awful scene, but he took it in stride, focusing only on his parents and me. I don't know how he could. The crowd was horrible.

"I love you, Caroline." He said, "I will do everything in my power to come home safe and sound. Then we can get married, just like we've always planned."

"You better."

We kissed before he turned to hug his mother and then his father. Then he followed the other passengers onto the airplane.

I stood with tears streaming down my face, his mother's arms around me. We held each other until his plane rolled away and out of sight.

Then it was their turn to leave me. We made our way through the terminal to their gate, where we said our goodbyes.

"Call me or write anytime, Caroline." His mother whispered to me, "We will get through this together."

Mr. Franks nodded and then escorted his wife to the plane. I stood there watching until their airplane was out of sight.

I felt numb as I mindlessly walked back through the airport and outside to the waiting taxis. I hailed one and headed home, softly crying the whole way.

Chapter Ten: January 1969

It had been about three months since Walter left, and I found myself sitting in a paper gown at my doctor's office. I had been feeling so sick. I was hungry all the time but couldn't eat. Tired but couldn't sleep. I figured it was the stress of having him gone, but my mother insisted I get checked. She was worried.

"Do I need to fly up there to take care of you?" She'd asked.

"No, I'm an adult, mother."

When any of us, my 3 brothers or myself, had been sick growing up, you would have thought the sky was falling. She would get all in a tizzy and haul us into the doctor. I started to hide when I felt sick, especially when I knew it was nothing because I didn't want to go to the doctor.

The only reason she found out I was sick this time was because she had come to visit me for a weekend. It's hard to hide when you spend so much time in the restroom. She almost didn't go home and had been threatening to come back since.

It wasn't until the nurse asked me questions about my illness that I realized.

"There is a chance I could be pregnant." Then, hearing myself say it out loud, I realized the truth in it, "Oh my, I think that might be it."

Now I was waiting for the doctor to confirm what I already knew. How could I not think of this sooner? Of course, that was it. I was pregnant. Walter and I had not been careful at all this last visit.

I have just been so distracted in my thoughts and missing him that I didn't realize.

"Hi, Caroline, it is good to see you. How're you doing?"

"I think I am feeling better. Thank you."

"Well, congratulations, you *are*, in fact, pregnant."

"Oh, that is wonderful news!" My mind really started racing. I would have a piece of Walter. It gave me such joy to think of.

The doctor examined me; confirmed that I was about 12 weeks along. We discussed my care and what I should be doing and not doing at this stage. It was all basic, standard instructions.

What a way to start the New Year. I practically floated home on a cloud, giddy and shocked, but he did confirm that the stress of the last several months is probably what messed me up. My menstrual cycle had been much lighter, but I still had one until this month as well, so who would have thought I'd get pregnant?

As soon as I got home, I pulled out my stationery so I could let Walter know our fantastic news. I was now regretting not marrying him before he left, but as soon as he came home, if even for a day, I was going to change that.

My dearest Walter,

I have just found out the most wonderful news. We are going to be parents! I just can't believe it. I get to have a little piece of you while you are gone. Then when you get back, we can be a little family. I am hoping for a boy that looks just like you. What do you think of the name Andrew?

I miss you so much, my love. The apartment feels so lonely without you and too big somehow, if you can imagine. I miss you the most on Sundays.

Take care, and please come back to me soon.

With all my love,

Caroline

I called my parents once I was done. I was so excited to tell them. My mother was less than thrilled with her only daughter having a baby out of wedlock.

"Caroline, what will people think?"

"I don't care what people think. Walter and I are in love and are engaged."

"And, you should have wed before he left. It's bad enough you have been living with him."

"I thought you supported my adventure and my courage."

"I do, did with your move to New York City, but living with a man is another story." She sighed, "I thought for sure you would be married by now and not pregnant. How will I be able to show my face around town or at church?"

"I think you will survive just fine, mother."

She put my father on the phone. He mostly grunted his replies, per usual. After that call, I didn't speak much to her for several weeks.

I could have been sleeping around like some other girls I knew. Walter had been my first and only boyfriend since I was 15, but that didn't matter to her. She only cared about what others thought, not her daughter's feelings.

Well, I supposed I was having this baby without her support then. But, after a few weeks, she called me up, and we talked things over.

"I apologize for my reaction to your news. I was surprised and also worried for you. Unfortunately, with Walter away, you will be raising the baby mostly on your own until he is back. It will be difficult."

"I know. I'm prepared for it, or I will be. I still have time to get ready."

"Maybe you should consider coming home. You can live with your father and me until Walter comes home. Then you can wed and become a family together."

I sighed. She had a point. It would be tough to work and pay for a babysitter. "That's a good idea. I will think about it."

"Good. I hope you do."

We continued our conversation, discussing my pregnancy so far and what I could expect soon. She told me about each of hers.

"And you were my easiest, so different from your brothers, and I just knew you had to be a girl. I only had a girl name picked out."

"Really? What if I would have been a boy?"

"We would have thought of something, but I just knew."

"I think this is a boy, and I'm thinking Andrew."

"That's so sweet. A mother is usually right."

With my mother happy and excited about the baby, I couldn't wait to hear from Walter.

I finally received my first letter from Walter at the beginning of February. It was a short letter, but it was marvelous to hear from him.

He said they were away from the action currently. The fighting was further north of where he was which made me feel better, and I hoped he stayed far, far away from it.

I grabbed the stack of letters I had been saving up, addressed them, and immediately ran to the postal box on the corner of our block. There was ice on the sidewalks, so I had to be extremely careful.

I kissed the stack of letters before slipping them into the postal box, saying a little prayer that they would reach him quickly. I was so anxious for him to hear about the baby and know he would be a father. I'm sure he would be as happy as I was, but I would be on pins and needles until I knew.

I decided not to tell anyone at work, only Mr. Butler since he was my boss, but I waited until late February to tell him. I was nearly 5 months along, and I would start to show soon. Luckily, it was winter, so I could wear a few layers of clothing and bulkier clothing.

"Congrats! Does Walter know yet?"

"I sent him a letter two, almost three weeks ago. I'm just not sure how long it takes mail to get there."

"Well, I am sure he will be pleased."

"I want to keep this confidential here in the office until either I know he knows or until I can't hide it any longer. Of course, you can tell Mrs. Butler." His wife was such a dear to me, always checking in on me, especially now that Walter was gone.

"Of course, when you are ready, I will let you start to tell people. I will tell Marie tonight. I'm sure she will be delighted for you."

When I was back at my desk, I felt a movement in my stomach. I had thought I had felt him before, but that was definitely a baby moving this time.

"Oh..." I put my hand on my stomach at the spot of impact. He was really in there. "Hi, Andrew," I whispered quietly.

Feeling the baby made me feel a lot less lonely at night and in that apartment. Over the next week, he was making his presence known more and more. I couldn't quite tell what he was doing in there, as it was mostly little flutters. Was that a kick or a punch? Did he roll or twist?

I talked to him nonstop at home, telling him how excited I was to meet him in a few months and how daddy was sorry he was away but that he would be home before we knew it.

I was starting to show, and it wouldn't be long before I couldn't hide it any longer. If a letter from Walter would confirm that he knew, I would happily tell the World. I would scream it from the rooftops.

Plus, my clothing was starting to get tight, and I couldn't wait to buy some cute little maternity tops and pants. My mother already had a few patterns to make me a few dresses.

I hadn't yet decided if I would move home or stay here; I wanted to hear from Walter before making any decisions. I hated that my life was almost in limbo waiting for Walter, and I was starting to really resent his choice.

Andrew would kick or move to remind me that we had love and would be a family soon.

"You are so right, Andrew." I said, "I just need to be patient."

Finally, the letter I had been waiting for arrived. I ran upstairs so I could read it.

Dearest Caroline,

I cannot believe it! I am going to be a father. You are going to be a mother. I am so happy. No, happy isn't the right word. I am over the moon with joy.

My only regret is that I am not there with you, and you have to go through all of this alone.

My darling, I would be the ideal partner. Running out in the middle of the night because you suddenly had a craving for pickles and ice cream or rubbing your feet after a rough day.

Do you think it will be a boy or a girl? I will be happy with either, as long as it has your beautiful blue eyes.

I love you and miss you desperately. Things here are indescribable and horrid. I wish, now, that I wouldn't have left you. I so hope one day you will forgive me for leaving you. When I get home, the first thing we will do is get married. I can't wait to make you Mrs. Walter James Franks.

I will write more soon.

With all my love,

Walter

I cried and laughed and then cried a little more. I was so happy to hear from him. He knew about our baby and was excited as I was.

I missed him deeply. He hadn't lost his Walter humor which I had to reread the part about ice cream and pickles, again and again, giggling each time. I knew he would be an excellent partner to me. He had been such a thoughtful boyfriend, always with a thoughtful gift, note, or gesture.

I grabbed my stationery to write him back. I wanted to get a reply to him as quickly as I could.

I told him all about my pregnancy so far.

"No insane cravings." I wrote.

I described the movements as best I could and how I had started to wear maternity clothing.

"I even bought a few things for the baby. Not many as I am thinking about moving home. I will need help, but I haven't decided yet. I really love my job here, and Sally mentioned that they could see me writing my own articles one day."

I included a recent picture of myself and a copy of one I had from his visit home with the two of us. I had the film developed right after he left, so he hadn't seen this one yet. I wrote on the back, *"Remember what you are fighting for."*

I meant to come home to our soon-to-be-born child and me. I was a week shy of 6 months. He would be home soon.

After I was finished, I checked out the window. It was icy out today, and it looked like it would snow again very soon. After the big snowstorm in February that shut down the city, I hoped we didn't have a repeat. Things had only gotten back to normal between the sanitation strike and the snowstorm – life here was messy.

I better get a move on if I was going to get this in the mailbox before the weather turned. I ran down the steps of our building, only to slip and slide down about 4 or 5 stairs to the bottom, hitting my rear on the sidewalk. I laughed and righted myself. A few people stopped to ensure I was safe.

"Thank you, I'm fine."

"You sure. Baby okay?" A sweet older lady asked.

I touched my stomach and felt him kick. "Everything seems okay."

"Well, don't hesitate to get checked out."

"Thank you."

I had an appointment with my doctor in a few days. I would likely be a little sore, but I felt fine. So I continued to the mailbox, dropping the letter in then checking the sky. There was still no snow, so I walked to the pizza place around the corner to grab a slice for dinner.

All seemed fine until I woke at 1 a.m. with extreme pains in my stomach, like cramps. It took my brain a moment too long to think of the cause.

"Noo...!"

I tried to get to the bathroom, but the pain was intense, and I doubled over with pain. When I finally got myself standing to walk to the restroom, I felt a warm liquid between my legs. It was blood. I called for an ambulance immediately.

Hours later, my beautiful baby boy was born. He was large for his age, nearly 2 pounds. The doctors and nurses were impressed.

"He's a fighter." The doctor told me after they had him stable in the neonatal unit, "He will be monitored around the clock. This is his best chance."

"He's so tiny." I mumbled, "When can I see him?"

"Soon. The nurse will take you down."

The doctor left, leaving me with my guilt and grief. I cried and cried, holding my now empty belly where my son was growing and healthy just a day ago. Now he had a long battle ahead of him, but the doctor confirmed this hospital had the best care for premature babies.

"You are in the best place for him and for you. Now rest as you have a long road ahead of you."

I had gotten a quick look at him before they took him away. He looked so much like Walter, just as I knew he would. He already had long eyelashes. I hadn't expected him to have eyelashes.

He also had ten long fingers and ten tiny little toes, and just like his father, he had one single dimple. Except for being born too soon, he was the perfect baby. If only I hadn't been so careless, he would still be kicking around in my stomach.

A few hours later, a nurse came in to wheel me down to see Andrew. He was in an incubator with wires and tubes all over him. He looked so tiny, so helpless.

"You can touch him through here." She told me.

I was so scared to touch him but more afraid not to. What if he didn't make it? He would think he was all alone.

I slipped my hands in the holes, and my hands were covered by the attached gloves.

"Andrew, sweetheart, it's mommy," I whispered. I touched his arm oh so softly. He startled a bit which caused me to jump back.

"He's okay. Babies jump like that sometimes. Try again." The nurse encouraged.

I touched his arm again, and this time he sighed. Tears formed in my eyes as I felt my child for the first time. The nurse stepped away to check on another baby and give me space.

I told him all about his daddy and how I couldn't wait to introduce them.

"You just have to fight for me. Be strong and grow." A lump stuck in my throat as I fought for words, "I'm so very sorry, Andrew. I'm so sorry I let you down."

I stayed with him as long as they let me, but soon I had to go back to my room. The doctors would be making the rounds shortly and need to check me.

"You can come back later." The nurse told me after we were back in my room, "And, I'll let you know if anything changes with him."

Three days later, I was visiting with Andrew. Though the staff had let me know they had a few close calls with him, he continued to fight hard for his life. I was so proud of him.

"Keep fighting, Andrew, keep fighting for me." I stroked his tiny arm, "Grandmother will be here tomorrow. She is flying in just to see you."

When I'd called to let her know about Andrew being born early, my mother said she would be here as soon as she could arrange it. I called each day to give an update until she could arrive.

As I was talking to Andrew, an alarm sounded, and I realized he had turned blue.

"Help, please help him."

Nurses came from around the room. They opened the incubator to work on him. His color finally improved, but he was clearly struggling.

Everything around was a blur; I had no idea what was said or what I should be doing. A doctor appeared from somewhere.

They were using all kinds of medical jargon, which made this all so confusing. I just stood by helpless while they worked on my tiny baby. His skin was gray, and he looked lifeless, but he made a slight noise here or there, so I had hope.

Finally, the doctor turned to me.

"I'm so sorry " I heard nothing else he said after that. I collapsed to the floor, howling and sobbing. A nurse helped me into a chair, rubbing my back and whispering to me.

"You can hold him if you'd like."

They handed him to me. Except for his coloring being a bit off, he looked perfect. I mumbled to him how sorry I was. He never had a chance at life because of my clumsiness.

"Oh, Andrew, you will forever be my angel now." I kissed him and held him close. Then they took him away, and I was all alone again.

Chapter Twelve: April 1969

My mother had been a godsend when she arrived the next day. She was my rock that I could anchor to and count on to hold me up.

She coordinated everything for Andrew. We had his body sent home to bury him at our family site.

Once that was handled, the next step was to make arrangements for me to go home with her for an extended stay and recuperate. It could be a month or more before I'd come back.

First, she called my landlord to let him know I would be gone for a short time. She'd worked out a payment plan with him. Since I usually paid in person, she arranged to send him a check through the mail. She then did the same with my utilities.

Finally, she called Mr. Butler to let him know and request time off for me. He understood and told me to take as much time as I needed. In a time when women would have gotten fired for a long break from work, I worked for a man and a company that valued me as an employee enough to give me what I needed.

In that moment, my lowest of all time, my mother was my hero. Of course, we didn't always see eye to eye, but I knew she had my back and loved me.

Today, she took me home to heal.

While staying with my parents, I didn't eat, barely slept, and didn't talk. I spent all my time crying in bed. I couldn't and didn't know how I would tell Walter. I'd failed him. I killed our son before he even had a chance at life, a chance to meet his father. I was a failure.

Then two weeks to the day of losing my little Andrew, Walter's father, Jack, came to the house. It was a rare day that I was out of bed and finally starting to cry a little less.

He and my father excused themselves to my father's study. I knew something was wrong, so I tip-toed down the hall. I stood outside the door, trying to hear.

"Jack, I don't know what she will do with the news. She just lost their baby. She is devastated."

"I know, and that's why I came to you first. My Gloria has taken to the bed just grief-stricken. I can't imagine what Caroline will say."

I stepped into the room, tears streaming down my face.

"Caroline.... I... I'm sorry." Jack bowed his head.

The sound that came out of me sounded like it came from somewhere else. I collapsed on the floor. Screaming his name over and over, banging my fist on the ground.

I cried for Andrew. I cried for Walter, and I cried for myself. Why was I being punished? I pleaded to the sky for this to be a bad dream.

I don't remember much, but at some point, my mother helped me from the floor and got me into bed. She gave me one of the sedatives that the doctor had prescribed and stayed by my bedside until I fell asleep.

Weeks went by before I remembered anything, and then another month before I could feel anything at all. I was so numb, and my heart was so broken.

My father, brothers, and Jack were heading to New York to clean out our apartment. I couldn't face it and was not going back. My current plan was to move home.

I overheard my mother giving my father detailed instructions.

"Be sure you save pictures and things that look special."

"All the pictures?"

"Yes, all of the pictures. There was that only vase that he gave her too. It was a simple thing, but I know she will want it. Of course, she will say she won't, but we need to save things because someday she will."

"Yes, dear."

"Make sure you pack those things separately from her clothes and items she will use right away. Be sure to label them, so there are no mix-ups."

"Anything else?"

"No, I think that is all for the apartment. Just be sure to see Mr. Butler to get her final paycheck and any personal items from her desk. He said he would have them."

"Okay. I have his number in my wallet."

"I just wish there was something I could do or say to make this better for her. There is no cure for a broken heart, and even time can't mend this one completely."

After they all left, my mother came and climbed into bed with me. She just wrapped her arms around me, and we cried. No words, just shared tears as she stroked my hair and my back. It was the best and worst feeling in the entire world.

It would be another month before I started to feel even remotely normal. It still hurt, and I couldn't say his name, but I could get out of bed. I could take a shower and put on clothes. I finally started to join my family for a meal and watch a few minutes of television without bursting into tears. It was a start.

The first time I left the house was nearly 3 months after getting the news about Walter. I was going to get my hair fixed with my mother. I was in fair spirits, and we chatted away like a mother and daughter might, well, when we weren't fighting.

As we drove from our home to the salon, I could feel my mood changing. We drove past several landmarks that sparked memories of Walter. The high school where we met and started our love affair, the bowling alley where we had so many dates, but when we went past the drive-in, I ended up crying uncontrollably, so my mother turned towards home.

The drive-in was where we spent the most memorable dates. It was where we first kissed. First time saying I love you and first made love in the back seat of his car. It had been awkward but also a wonderful, beautiful experience.

When we got home, I ran to my bed and cried. A few hours later, my mom came in with a cup of hot tea. She climbed into bed next to me, held my hand, and stroked my hair, something she was doing a lot these days. It was such a comfort.

"Oh, mama, I should have married him. I should have married him. Why didn't I listen to him or you ....or anyone? I love him so much; how can he just be... gone? And my baby... my baby is gone too...." I choked.

"I don't know. Sometimes life doesn't make sense and isn't fair. There isn't always a reason why things happen."

"I wish you could have seen Andrew. He was so tiny, but he looked so much like Walter. He had tiny little fingers and toes and the cutest little button nose. I wanted him so much."

We were silent for a few moments. Both with quiet tears running down our faces.

"I lost a baby once. Not as far along as you were, but the sadness of it was heartbreaking. People tried to tell me that I had three healthy boys, I should feel blessed. But I felt like our family wasn't complete yet. I know it isn't what you are going through, but I understand some of the feelings."

"I didn't know that."

"It was right before I got pregnant with you. Like I said, I just felt like our family wasn't complete, and it wasn't until you were here. When I lost that baby, I lost faith in life and lost hope. You made me believe in miracles again." She paused, "Sounds a little dramatic, but the point is your miracle is out there to be found. You will find your hope, your purpose, and the meaning in all of this. It will just take some time and patience."

I didn't know it at the time, but it would be nearly 50 years before I truly understood what she meant.

Chapter Thirteen: October 1969

I'd been here about six months, and I was slowly starting to feel better. The grief was still raw, but I could function, and the tears didn't flow as easily. At only 20 years old, I felt I had matured at least ten years between the loss of my boyfriend and my son.

I'd recently secured a position as a typist for our local newspaper. Not as glamorous as my position at Groove Fashion. But it had helped distract my mind, and I didn't sit around the house deep in depression.

However, I really missed the job and my life in New York. I wanted it all back, including Walter and Andrew.

Knowing that couldn't happen, I had to make some tough decisions so I could move forward again with life. So today, I was flying to New York City to meet with the Butlers.

We had kept in touch since I left New York. Marie Butler called me a few times a week to check on me. They had sent cards and even came to visit once.

I wanted to thank them in person, again, for all the support they have given me over the past several months. We were also going to discuss my return to the magazine.

As I walked from the hotel to the restaurant, I saw a group of war protesters. At the same time, I noticed a soldier walking not far away from them. The protesters ran up to him and started chanting and yelling at him, their faces red with anger.

I was scared for him, but he took it in stride, as Walter had done, and just continued to walk on. He never blinked or flinched at them. He just walked on head high.

The protesters didn't follow him but continued to taunt him and yell. It rattled me to my core as I remembered how I had felt hearing some like them yelling at Walter.

I understood the protesters' point of view in a way, and I agreed, but they forgot that these were people. Most of these soldiers were just following orders, trying to live their lives as best as they could. They needed and deserved to have our support and love. I didn't know yet what I would do, but I knew I had to do something for them.

I hurried on to the restaurant and far from the enraged crowd. By the time I arrived, I had several ideas and thoughts swirling around in my head.

As my eyes adjusted to the darker interior of the restaurant, I scanned the random faces looking for the Butlers. They were seated near a window, so I manipulated my way through the restaurant to the table.

"Caroline, dear, you look wonderful." Mrs. Butler gushed as she gave me a hug.

She smelled faintly of powder and the latest perfume from Chanel. She was dressed in a peach pants suit with pearls. Her hair was perfectly styled as if she had just come from her hairdresser. She was the picture of style and elegance. Most people would think she was a rich snob, but she was the most caring, loving, and generous person.

"Hi, Mrs. Butler, you look ... stunning." Why did I say that? Well, it was the truth.

"Oh, thank you, and darling, please call me Marie. After all, we have cried together."

"Caroline, good to see you." Mr. Butler gave me a quick hug and a kiss on the cheek.

"You too, sir."

"Sir?" He said with a chuckle, "Thank you, but you don't work for me any longer, at least not currently; please call me Gene, and as my beautiful wife said, we have shared a lot over the past few months."

"Habit, Gene." I tested out the new name.

The waiter came over to take my drink order. The Butlers had white wine, so I ordered the same. I scanned the menu; everything sounded terrific.

"What do you all recommend here?"

"Oh, everything is delicious here, but I like the roast beef, and he likes the sausage stuffed flank steak."

We discussed some other items on the menu before the waiter returned. He took our orders and then left us to visit.

"So how have you been?" Marie reached over and squeezed my hand.

"I'm... well I'm doing okay. It's still tough. Being in New York has sparked so many memories, even more than being at home."

"I'm sure it will be that way for a while. I would be lost without Gene." They looked at each other for just a moment. You could feel the love between them. My heart pulled a little.

"How is Richard? Has he returned yet?" Their son Richard had been injured in battle and would soon return to the states.

Thankfully, he wasn't so severely injured that he couldn't enjoy life, or the best he could, considering what he's been through.

"He should be on a plane heading back as we speak."

"I'm so happy for you all. I know it has been difficult waiting on him." As happy as I was for them, my heart tightened, and I could almost hear it cry for Walter. "So, on my way over today, I had an idea...."

I explained about the protesters and the soldier. His reaction was professional, but I am sure it tore at his heart and beat him down.

"It broke my heart. I remember Walt getting the same treatment, and none of them should deal with this alone. So I want to create an organization to help support troops when they return. I know there is the VA already and other organizations, but I feel like we could do some things differently. They are overworked, and our project could help reduce their load. We'd give vets extra resources to help them transition back into civilian life."

"That is an interesting idea. We have all heard about the emotional and physical scars of those returning, but then to be harassed and treated like trash is just not necessary. It was the government's choice to get in this war, agree or disagree with it; those boys and girls should not be treated like that when they return."

"Our Richard is returning, and I hate the thought of him being treated like that. He has been through enough." Marie said.

"That is exactly why I want to do this. I don't know exactly how or what it will all encompass yet, but I have to do something, and I think there is a good idea in here somewhere."

Our food arrived; we continued to discuss plans as we ate. They were right about the food here. The roast beef just about melted in my mouth. After eating, we ordered another glass of wine to continue our conversation.

"Well, I am all in. I can provide financial support, and I have several contacts. I know I run a fashion magazine but believe it or not, I have a lot of ties with politicians and various city officials. It's good to have friends in high places." He added with a wink.

We walked out of the restaurant and into the bright lights and chaos of the New York streets. The vibe here always pumped me up. I felt like I could do big things

"Thank you both so much for lunch. It was wonderful; the food and the company."

"It was our pleasure, dear." She kissed my cheek, and we hugged, "We will be in touch about the new organization. I'm excited about it and can't wait to help."

"I will, Marie, and let me know when Richard gets in."

Gene and I hugged and said goodbye. They turned, walking away hand in hand. I watched them for a moment, looking away before the tears started. Would my heart ever heal from the loss?

I walked fast to the subway, trying to walk the pain away, forcing myself to think about the exciting new organization I would be creating in Walter's memory.

Chapter Fourteen: January 1970

A new year, a new decade, and an all-new Caroline. I moved back to New York City, not far from my first apartment.

I had been able to bring my bedroom furniture from home this time, and I still had a few things from my first apartment.

In addition, I found a lovely sofa and side chair in shades of green and beige. I added a few end tables and a funky glass lamp to complete the living room. This kitchen had a bar, so I found two high-back leather stools to add to it.

The place felt comfortable and homey, and even though some things had been bought for my life with Walt, it felt vastly different here in this new place and in this arrangement. Just what I needed for this latest chapter of my life.

It took us several months to get things going, but I officially launched the Walter J. Franks Veteran's Support Foundation in January 1970. We were currently only open in New York, but if it caught on, we hoped to expand into other cities.

The Butlers had been invaluable in getting this up and running. When Gene said he had friends in high places, he was not exaggerating. He knew the mayor, several congressmen, and senators.

He also had some friends who were tied to the military. It really helped us work with the Veterans Affairs directly. We weren't trying to compete with or replace them but be additional support for our troops and help ease their load at the VA.

His connections helped us open in record time, if even in a small capacity. I was simply happy to be doing something to help others and give back, all in memory of Walter. It sure beats wallowing in my sorrow.

I hired various physiologists, transition, and financial counselors. There was a department to help with resume building and provide interview training. The same department helped them with placement, getting their foot in the doors of companies that wouldn't look at them without help. It was all coming together.

Since the war was in full force at this point, we mostly had soldiers returning that had been injured. These soldiers got more help at the VA offices than ours. Due to this, a lot of our initial work was attending protests and staging our own.

We wanted to show a different point of view. So we printed flyers talking about our message, one of support for the troops while still not supporting the war, a message we hoped would catch on.

At first, we were met with negative responses, threats, trash, and boos. But with time, the negative was replaced with more of a neutral reaction or indifference to us. I knew we hadn't changed minds, but I hoped it made them think about the soldiers as people.

We also found out when troops would be arriving at the airports, and we'd show up with welcome home banners and balloons. We cheered loudly and tried to act as a buffer against the angry mobs.

We watched a lot of news and read a lot of newspapers to help us learn anything about troops coming back or facts about the war itself. It helped us support them. Of course, we didn't have the same experience, but we knew the stories and could relate to the facts and knowledge.

As the president started to pull more and more troops from the war, and as we got a clearer vision of the work and support that was needed to our troops, our office became busier.

Most of us started working 12 to 14-hour days. I did it to forget but seeing all the soldiers returning, it really hit home that Walter was never coming home. I threw myself even more into my work, so I wasn't alone and had little time to think about it.

One day I met one of the first women to come in for services. I knew that there were women in the war zone, but we had yet to have one come through our office. She was about my age, not married, and had no children. She had seen a lot of violence and more than her fair share of the consequences of that violence. She had been a nurse in one of the most active areas.

I wanted to interview her myself to understand if we were providing the correct services for women. I greeted her in the reception area.

"Hi, Francine? I'm Caroline Graham."

"Hi, yes, that's me." She shook my hand, "And please call me Frannie."

"Okay, Frannie, please follow me to my office."

As we walked to my office, I offered coffee or water. She declined.

"Please, have a seat." I sat behind my desk, and she took the chair across. "How are you finding our services?"

"So far, everyone has been helpful, caring, and providing great resources."

"That's wonderful to hear. I like to meet with as many of our clients as possible. I think you are one of the first women that we have seen."

"Is that so? Well, I know several and will spread the word."

"Thank you. That would be great. We like to help as many as we can. Our mission is to make the transition as smooth as possible."

"I think it's a good thing you are all doing here. I had gone to the VA offices. They're just overwhelmed, plus all the protests all over town... It's crazy out there."

"I know. We try to attend, when possible, to show support, but we have gotten busier." I smiled, "Speaking of, I am always looking for ways to improve. Are there any services that you can think of we are missing for women?"

"Well, I'm not sure as I don't have children, but some do, maybe counseling for families?"

"Oh, that's a good idea. Unfortunately, we only have counseling and departments to support service members now."

We talked for nearly an hour more. I ended up canceling my next two appointments to keep talking to her. She was like a long-lost friend. I then did something I hadn't done in a long time; I left work early so that Frannie and I could go to dinner together.

"So, are you from New York?" I asked her as we sipped our wine.

"Not exactly. We moved a lot. My family is currently in New Jersey. Also, I have a good friend, Susan. She is from here and suggested I come out here, so here I am." She smiled, "What about you?"

"I moved here a couple of years ago with my boyfriend."

"Oh, nice."

I was glad she didn't push for more information, at least not yet. I wasn't ready to talk about it, only wanting to get to know my new friend.

After dinner, we went to a local nightclub for drinks and dancing. It was the perfect night out.

From that point forward, we were the best of friends. She renewed my faith in life outside of work. We spent a lot of time together.

We actually had a spot open in the organization that she could fill. She quickly became a great addition to our organization and helped get our spouse and family counseling services up and running.

Chapter Fifteen: March 1970

It had been about a month since I first met Frannie. She had recently started working at the Foundation. Her idea to create a spouse and family support department was in the planning stages, so I got to work with her nearly daily. It gave us a lot of time to get to know each other.

She made me go to lunch, something I was famous for skipping. Often, I worked from sunup to sundown without much of a break. Why? It helped combat the loneliness, and by the time I got home each evening, I was too exhausted to notice the hole missing in my life.

While I did have a few girlfriends growing up, we'd grown apart since I moved away, and they started families. We did keep in touch by sending letters to each other a few times a week. Dottie and I had a twice-monthly phone call. No matter what else was going on, we made that call. Sometimes she only had time for a quick one because of her children, but it was nice to hear her familiar voice.

My friendship with Frannie was different, though. She was not from my old chapter of life and had brought fun energy into my day. She was fresh and new.

"Everyone's getting settled in the conference room," my secretary, Judith, said at my office door.

"Oh, is it time already? I'll be right there." I smiled at her.

I grabbed my notepad, flipped to yesterday's meeting notes, and did a quick review. Then I grabbed my pen and coffee mug before heading down the hall to the conference room for our weekly staff meeting.

"Hey, Caroline," Frannie said and then gestured to the chair next to her.

"Hey," I took a seat next to her. "Alright, team, are we ready to start today's meeting?"

"Yes," Mike said. He was the vice-president and a veteran himself, "So from our last meeting, I had an action to work with Frannie on the classified ads so we could start hiring staff. To update, we have it drafted and ready to go when you say the word."

He slid a copy of the ad over to me. I read it, made a few correction notes, and passed it back. He reviewed my notes and nodded

"Always the editor," Frannie said with a laugh.

"I can't help it." I shrugged, "Okay next order of business. Office space."

"The floor plan for the 8th floor has been approved by the city, and we can move forward," Jerry said. He was in charge of the building. "We should be able to start early next week. I'm just lining up the contractors now."

"Perfect. It will be exciting to see that space come together."

We continued to each item on our list. Everyone giving updates or asking questions. We created our next list of actions and then wrapped the meeting.

"Well, thank you, team. This all sounds wonderful, and I believe we'll make our target dates to have this all complete. Again, I appreciate everyone's work."

As everyone gathered their things to go, Frannie turned to me.

"Lunch?"

"Hm, I have a lot to do."

"Oh, come on. You always say that, and then you always go and somehow get all your tasks done."

"Fine." I laughed. "The diner?"

"Of course!"

The diner was a quick walk a few blocks from the office. They had the best lunch specials. We grabbed our pocketbooks and coats, then minutes later, we were walking out of the building.

"Oh, chilly today," I noted, pulling my coat a bit tighter.

"Yeah." But she seemed unfazed by it. "You aren't going to back out on me tonight, are you?"

"No, I'm still planning to go with you."

"Good. You put me off last time."

"I'm going. I'm going." I hooked my arm with hers, and we continued to the diner.

There was a jazz band that we both enjoyed. They were playing at a bar not far from us. The plan was to go out for dinner first and a few drinks while listening to the beautiful music.

Arriving at the restaurant, our favorite waitress, Doris, greeted us. We ordered club sandwiches and handmade chips.

"Extra pickle with mine, please," Frannie said.

"Of course, suga'."

Doris was a sweet older lady who looked like she'd had a tough life, from the deep wrinkles in her face to the limp in her stride. But she always had a smile and a kind word. She was who I strived to be when I grew older.

"I think the department is coming together nicely," Frannie said.

"Yes, I think so too." I sipped the drink that Doris had just dropped off, "Everyone is hitting the project deadlines, and if that continues, we will be up and running with this new division next month."

"That is exciting to think about." She smiled, "Thanks for taking a chance on hiring me."

"Aw, you're welcome. Thanks for being such a great friend to me."

"Ha, if I was a better friend, I wouldn't let you get away with standing me up so often."

"Not this again." I laughed.

"Yes, this again." She giggled.

"I'm going tonight. I promise."

"Good. I'm not taking no this time. It's the Coleman Trio."

"Oh, I love them," Doris said as she came over with our meals. "They are playing over at Jazz Notes, right?"

"Yes, tonight," Fran said with a smile.

"I might go myself."

"Tickets are sold out," I said.

"Oh, honey, I may look like an old lady working in this rundown ole diner, but I have magic powers." She winked and left to go help the next table.

"I want to be her when I grow up," Frannie said, watching the older lady dart from table to table, refilling drinks or greeting a regular.

"I was just thinking the same thing."

"That's why we're such good friends." She said with a laugh.

We finished our lunch and then said goodbye to Doris.

"See you tonight, darlings." She waved as we went out the door.

We stepped into the flow of foot traffic and started to walk back towards the building. The crowds made me feel energized and motivated me to work hard. With each step, I could feel the beat of the city.

"We should skip the rest of the day and go shopping," Frannie said.

I could see our building. We were almost back in the work zone.

"I can't skip work, and neither can you. We have deadlines."

"Pish-posh, we'll meet the deadlines even taking a few hours off. It's just one day."

I searched her face for any hint that this was a bad idea. I felt my resolve slip as she grinned.

"You are such a bad influence on me." I grabbed her arm, and we turned towards the bus stop. The final destination was shopping.

"You know you love me." She chuckled as she let me drag her along.

She was actually a positive influence on me. Without her, I would work too much and have no fun. She grounded me, always told it like it was, and forced me out of my comfort zone.

Chapter Sixteen: April 1970

It has been just over a year since my life changed, losing my one true love and my precious son. So I decided to make a trip home and spend some time with my family and the Franks, so we could remember them both. And even though I had only a few short months with Andrew, he took up a huge part of my heart.

"Are you sure you want me to come?" Frannie asked.

"Yes, please." I said, "It's going to be difficult at times, but I think having you there will keep me grounded."

"I didn't know either of them, and we've only been friends a short time. Are you sure?"

"I am."

She stared at me a moment, "Alright, I'll come, but only because I need a few days away."

With that settled, we made our plans, buying plane tickets and planning for time off of work. We'd be staying with my parents.

It was a smooth trip, and once we landed, we were greeted at the gate by my parents. My mother rushed to me, wrapping me in a hug.

"Mom, Dad, this is my friend, Frannie."

"Nice to meet you, Mr. and Mrs. Graham," Frannie said.

"Oh please, call me Connie." My mother said.

My dad mumbled his greeting and his request for him to be called Dale. I smiled at Frannie. She had already been warned that my father would be quiet, though he spoke when necessary.

We loaded our bags into the trunk, and my dad drove us home. I pointed out all the sights to Frannie. Not that our town had tourist spots, but my high school, my favorite diner, and the drive-in.

"It's just how you described it, Caroline." Frannie said, "Cute."

"Besides the memorial, what are plans while you're home?" My mother asked.

"Not much. We have the memorial tomorrow, and then we will likely go hang out at Silver's." It was the local bar where we were going to meet a couple of my childhood girlfriends, "We'll be meeting up with Dottie and Karen."

"Oh, that will be nice for you girls." Mom said, "I have a pot roast for dinner tonight, and then all the catering is set up for tomorrow. The Franks should be over by 10, and then we will head over to the cemetery."

"Sounds good." My stomach twisted thinking about tomorrow.

I wanted this. Heck, it was my idea, but I was still anxious. I had come a long way in a year, but it was mostly by avoidance and throwing myself into my work.

We pulled up at my childhood home, and the stress of life melted away. Home meant security and protection, my soft place to fall when things got tough.

My parents had set up two of the upstairs bedrooms as guest rooms. Frannie took the one next to my room, and I took my old bedroom, now a guest room. There was no evidence that it had ever been my bedroom.

My pink floral wallpaper had been scrapped, and it was repapered with jewel colors stripes. All the furniture was replaced with dark wood pieces while mine growing up had been white.

"Your house is wonderful, Connie," Frannie said as my mom gave her the tour.

"Thank you, dear. Though with all my children grown, it is starting to feel too big."

"Might be time to sell." My father said in one of his rare moments of speaking up.

"Maybe so." My mother said.

"What? You can't sell." I said. How could they even consider that? Where would I go when life got too complicated?

"It's time." Dad said, "We don't need all this space. Your brothers seldom come home. You have your life going again, so why not?"

He had a point, but I didn't like it. Nowhere else would feel like coming home, not like this place. I looked around, taking it all in. This could be the last time I sat here in my family home, sharing a special moment with my parents.

"I guess that makes sense, but where will you live?"

"They are building some new smaller homes across town, and we have been looking at them."

"You've been thinking about this for a while?"

"Yes. We are actually putting the house on the market after your visit."

"When were you going to tell me?"

"Now." My father said.

I guess there wasn't anything I could say to change their minds. His tone sounded final.

"We will leave you girls to unpack. I'll go get dinner warming. Come down when you are done." Mom chirped.

After they left, I shrugged at Frannie, "I'm sorry for that. I didn't know... " I could feel a lump forming in my throat.

"I'm sorry. I probably shouldn't have come. I already knew it was going to be an emotional weekend for you, but I know how much home means to you."

"Thanks, but no, I need a friend here."

While I'd kept in touch with a few of my childhood friends, I didn't have many people that I was close to. When I worked at Groove, I didn't spend much time with the other girls, only at lunch and an odd night out. Nobody I would call in an emergency or if I needed to talk.

Then when Walter was alive, we had a few friends that he worked with that we'd go out with on occasion, but when he was fired and then enlisted, he hadn't kept in touch, and I definitely hadn't.

With Frannie, I felt a different friendship with her. We just clicked from the first meeting, and we spent nearly every day together since she started working at the foundation. Then a lot of nights, we'd go straight to dinner or a bar. Sometimes we ate at my apartment, sometimes hers.

She was someone I knew I could count on, and I really wanted to share this with her. If she stood by me through this trip, we'd be lifelong friends.

She went to her room to unpack and then freshen up a bit while I did the same in my room. We agreed to join back up when we were both finished.

I looked around at my old room. I already missed the pale pink wallpaper. But, the delicate flowers were forever in my mind. All the nights, I would stare at the print as I'd fall asleep.

I walked to the window to look out at my backyard. My mother's perfectly landscaped yard with the roses, hydrangeas, and azaleas at least hadn't changed. I'd spent so many hours helping her and smelling those beautiful blooms as a small child.

How could they sell my childhood? I sighed, but maybe it was time for us all to have a fresh start.

"Knock, knock," She said at my door, "I'm done. How about you?"

"Yes, just finished."

"I see why you like it here. It's nice. My house growing up was not like this. We moved a lot and lived wherever we could."

"I'm sorry."

"No, no reason to be sorry. It was not a bad life, just had no place to call home. So home became the place my mother and sister were."

She smiled. I reached forward to squeeze her hand in support. "Well, let's go eat. My mom's pot roast is the best."

The next day was the memorial. While I wanted to remember, I could also feel my emotions swirling. The pain was still so raw, so crushing. My heart still ached for them both. I failed to protect Andrew and Walter, who had been so full of life the last time I saw him. I could still hear his laugh, see his smile with his lone dimple, and smell his soap. He should never have been in that place.

I cried quietly in my bed all night. Today, I was trying to put on a brave face, be an adult about all of this, but both of them should be here. We should be celebrating, not memorializing them. I wanted to throw a tantrum, curse, scream, but it wouldn't change the fact that they were both gone.

I dressed with extra care wanting to look my best to celebrate the lives of two people that meant the most to me. I'd asked my mother to make me a new dress in the same ice blue material that I'd worn to the winter formal all those years ago.

It wasn't a somber color, but I didn't want it to be a depressing day, even though I knew there would be sadness. But the ice blue dress was a sweet memory for me, and I wanted a piece of it with me today.

I fastened a small gold locket around my neck. Touching it as I remembered the Christmas that Walter had given it to me. I opened it to see our faces together. He was so handsome, so young.

"Oh Walter, I miss you more each day," I said; then, I looked up at myself and smiled weakly at my reflection. I then went downstairs to join my family and to find Frannie.

The Franks arrived promptly at 10 am as promised. We would meet my brothers and my sister-in-law at the cemetery.

"Oh, Caroline, dear, you look wonderful." Mrs. Franks gushed as she hugged me.

"Thank you, Mrs. Franks. You look beautiful as always." I smiled, "How are you feeling?"

"Honestly, I'm dreading this and looking forward to it at the same time. I move through my whole day as before, but a huge hole has been ripped out of my life." She pulled out a tissue and dabbed at her eyes, "But, I'm so thankful to have this chance to celebrate Walt and your sweet Andrew. I'm sorry I never got to meet him."

"Me too." I had a few pictures of him in the incubator and a soft yellow blanket that he never got to use. Those were the only signs that he ever existed. "I want to introduce you to my good friend. This is Frannie. Frannie, this is Walter's mother."

"Nice to meet you, Mrs. Franks."

"Nice to meet you too."

"And this is Mr. Franks."

He greeted her with a hardy handshake, "Nice to meet you, Frannie, and any friend of Caroline's is a friend of ours."

"Are we ready to head over?" My dad asked.

We all agreed. The Franks went in their car. My parents, Frannie and I went in my family's car.

Even with my blue dress, the mood was solemn as we drove over. I watched the familiar sights of my hometown go by from the back seat. It all blurred together as my eyes filled with tears. I rubbed at the fabric for comfort and to remember.

I peeked at Frannie. She was stoic, but it was a comfort to have my friend here with me. Someone who wasn't a part of this chapter of my life so she could be impartial and not emotionally invested in the grief of these two people. Somehow that fact alone held me together.

Why? Because even though Walter and Andrew had been huge parts of my life, Frannie's presence here showed me that the world around me went on. She and her friendship gave me hope that I could move forward with my life and someday find happiness again.

The weather had been iffy, but the rain started as we pulled into the cemetery. It really set the mood for all of us. As if heaven was crying with us. So much for not having a depressing day.

My father drove around to their headstone. They shared one and were buried with the rest of the Franks' ancestors. Father and son together forever. I had already made plans to be buried here with them. His parents insisted.

My mother had advised that I wait in case I got married someday. I argued that I wanted to be near my son. She simply nodded and didn't bring it up again.

I could see that there were people already standing nearby. It looked like Larry and Mary Jane, along with Karl and his girlfriend, Jan, and then Dean, playing with Denise Ann.

I hadn't seen her since Christmas. She had grown so much. Her dark hair was pulled into two pigtails tied with bright blue ribbons that matched her gingham blue dress.

Andrew would have been born less than a year after her. Though my brother and I weren't close, I daydreamed about the two cousins playing and growing up together. They would run around during holidays, giggling and chasing each other.

Dad put the car in park at the curb. Then we joined my brothers at the gravesite. Larry came forward to put his arms around me.

"You okay?" He whispered.

"Yeah." Though I was only hanging on by a thread at the moment, I wanted to do this.

I set down the roses on their headstone. Then looked around at the faces of my amazing support system. It was the only reason I had been able to get back to a somewhat normal life.

"Thank you all for coming today. It means so much that you have come not only to support me but to remember the two people that meant the world to me." I continued my speech, talking about Walter and my short time with Andrew. I stammered and choked on tears through the entire thing. "Again, thank you from the bottom of my heart. Mr. Franks, did you want to say something?"

He began speaking, but I'll be honest, I didn't hear what he said. Tears streamed down my face as I looked down at the names etched in the dark gray granite, Walter James Franks and Andrew Walter Franks. Father and son who never met, resting together now side by side for eternity.

Frannie put her arm around me. It was comforting and grounding in the moment and slowed the stream of tears.

After Mr. Franks, Mrs. Franks said a few things, and then one of Walter's childhood friends, James, spoke.

"Walt was one of a kind, man. He was caring, funny, and always happy to lend a hand. The world lost a good soul when Walter passed." He nodded and hung his head.

Once everyone had their turn, my dad invited everyone to our house for lunch. We had a full catered meal waiting at home.

I was exhausted by the end of the day, but it felt good to remember them. It felt good to have some peace. Though I knew the pain wouldn't end here, it was still a positive step for me.

Chapter Seventeen: May 1972

As life does, it keeps moving forward, and the earth keeps spinning. The pain in my heart wasn't as fresh. But, as time is said to do, it heals all wounds.

Instead of looking to the past and what could have, I focused on the Foundation and my friendships. My most important of those was Frannie.

We decided to move in together and found a small two-bedroom, one bathroom on the Upper West Side, not far from my first apartment. This area was full of memories, but it was also oddly comforting with the familiar streets, stores, restaurants, and even some of the same faces.

It was nice to have someone to talk to and not be alone, but we each had our own space when we wanted alone time. It was the perfect situation.

We were alike in so many ways. Both neat and tidy. We both loved to cook and often cooked together, especially baking cookies or cakes. Frannie made the best cakes.

But the biggest difference between us was that she liked to go out, but most nights, I preferred to stay in and read or watch television or both. I liked a quiet life.

However, some nights she could convince me to go with her. It was almost always the same argument, and sometimes I fell for it.

"Come on, Caroline, you never want to go out, and it has been a few years since Walter passed. You need to meet a new guy!"

She was one of the few people that could say this, and it didn't bother me.

"But I just... I'm not sure that I am ready."

"I know I didn't know him, but from all you have told me about him, I can honestly say this, he would want you to be happy and meet someone else." She reached over and squeezed my hand, "Plus, I can't go alone."

"Fine, fine. You're probably right. Walter wouldn't want me to mourn forever." I squeezed her hand back, "It has been a long time."

"We should go shopping! If you find the perfect outfit, you'll feel more confident."

"Well, you know I am always ready for some shopping."

We headed to our favorite resale boutique shop. I always found the best outfits here.

Today was no exception. I found several things, but my favorite was a gorgeous gold and green paisley jumpsuit. So this is what I decided to wear out tonight.

When we got home, I curled my hair into a large wavy mane that framed my face, then I applied a touch of mascara, a little eye shadow, and shiny red lipstick.

Was I ready to meet someone new? I couldn't help but think about Walter. What would he think? Honestly, I knew the answer, and everyone was right. He loved me and wouldn't want me to be unhappy forever.

"I love you, Walt. I always will." I said to the mirror and waited for an answer that never came. I took it as a sign.

Frannie wasn't the only one telling me I needed to meet someone. Every conversation with my mother started out with that same sentiment.

"So, Caroline, have you met anyone new and interesting lately?"

I would always answer in the same way. "Oh yes, there was this nice older woman on the bus today. I gave her my seat, and she shared a peppermint with me."

"Caroline Marie Graham, you know what I mean. Why can't you give me a straight answer?"

"Because I'm not ready to meet anyone or date. Walter was my world. I'm just not there yet."

"Do you want to grow old alone?"

"No, I want to grow old with Walter, but since that isn't an option now, I pick old and alone."

"I just don't know what to say to you anymore."

This conversation had a few variations, but the basic idea was the same. Caroline was going to grow old alone, and honestly, I was okay with it, my mother not so much.

I wasn't as okay with it as I tried to make my mother and friends believe. Most nights, I cried myself to sleep. I cried for my little boy and for my never-to-be husband. The number of times I could kick myself for not marrying him before he left were innumerable. It was almost a daily regret.

The truth was, though, I had been on a few dates. Nothing serious and were typically a lunch date. There is no kiss good night, rarely a second date, and no reason to tell anyone. Frannie knew about them since we worked together, but she also knew it wasn't worth mentioning.

Frannie and I arrived at the nightclub around 11, just as things were starting to get hopping. It was loud and crowded, and that was just on the outside. I had a moment of panic as we waited, and I almost turned to run.

Frannie hooked her arm with mine, "Oh no, you don't. You look stunning, and you, my dear, are going in."

We made our way through the door and into the hustle and bustle of the club. The bright, flashing lights and smoke momentarily blinded me. However, soon the beat of the music and the laughing, happy vibe from the crowd drew me in. I really did need this from time to time.

We headed to the bar to grab a cocktail. We sipped our drinks as we scanned the room. Everyone was dressed to the nines. Lots of bell bottoms, jumpsuits, empire dresses, and some of the newer miniskirts paired with boots.

Even though I'd left Groove magazine, I still bought it and always kept an eye on the latest and greatest in fashion.

The band played all the hits, and the dance floor was hopping. While sipping our drinks, Frannie and I swayed and sang along with the music.

"This band is good," I commented.

"Yeah, they are." Frannie said, "Let's make a loop. See if any cute boys are here."

I nodded, and we bopped our way through the crowd, making a complete loop around the club, ending up back near the bar. There were quite a few cute men tonight, but none that piqued my interest.

"Wanna dance?" She asked, gesturing towards the dance floor.

"Sure."

We set our now empty glasses on the edge of the bar and then made our way to the dance floor. It was full of both couples and singles.

We danced nearly non-stop until the heat and moving bodies got to me.

As if reading my mind, Frannie fanned herself and mouthed she was hot, so we exited the dance floor and headed back to the bar. We ordered another round of drinks and then wandered around until we found some people getting up from a table. So we claimed it for a much-needed break.

"Thank you for dragging me out. This is fun!" I shouted above the music.

"Anytime. You work too hard."

We both laughed at that. She was right, of course.

"Yes, sadly, that is true, but you have helped me get out more."

"Well, I think Walter would be proud of you tonight." She smiled and held her glass up to toast. I clinked my glass with hers.

The music and crowd noise made it hard for much more conversation, so we just enjoyed the band and our drinks. We occasionally would comment on this person or that couple, a girl's outfit that looked cute or that one that didn't.

"So, don't look now, but there is a guy over there checking me out." She flipped her short hair a little and smiled his way.

"Oh, really? Are you sure he's looking at you?" I teased. I turned slightly and as casually as possible, trying to make it look like I was just scanning the room, not really looking at him, "Oh, Fran, he is hot. Go say hi!"

"Nay, I'm old-fashioned. He needs to come to me. Oh, and he is." She smoothed her dress, trying to act casual while looking around but not directly at him.

"Hi there. I'm Norm, and you are?"

"Frannie, and this is my friend Caroline."

"Well, hi, ladies. Can I buy you a fresh drink?" He asked as he gestured to our drinks.

"Why, thank you. Yes, that would be nice," Frannie said.

"I'll be right back." He headed to the bar and returned with his drinks and a friend in a blink. "This is Luis. We were in the Army together. Luis, this is Caroline and Frannie."

"Evenin', ladies," Luis said.

He had an easy smile and dark eyes you could get lost in. His hair was cut short to his head, and his bell-bottom corduroy pants and a button-down shirt with a striped pattern looked brand new.

Working at the Foundation with recently discharged veterans, I had gotten good at spotting those freshly back. New clothes, stiff posture, and a bit jumpy were all signs. He had two of the three going for him.

"Hello." Fran and I said in near unison.

We made small talk while drinking fresh drinks, well Fran and Norm talked, while Luis and I listened and spoke only if we were addressed.

"Wanna hit the dance floor?" Norm asked after we'd finished our drinks.

"Let's do it," Frannie said eagerly.

He reached his hand out and pulled her along with him to the dance floor.

Luis looked at me, flashing a slight smile, then nodded his head to follow them. I did so I wasn't rude and out of loyalty to my friend.

Watching Norm and Frannie, I thought they looked so natural together, as if they had known each other for years rather than just an hour. She laughed at something he said, and he had a grin as he guided her around the dance floor.

I watched them together with a bit of jealousy, then instantly felt a ping of guilt for Luis. We'd been paired together only due to our friends' interest, so I shouldn't feel guilty. It wasn't like I picked him out of the room and then ignored him.

Still, I mentally shook off my negative thoughts and pulled my attention back to him. Smiling at him, I tried to keep my mind in the present. But the pinched expression on his face told me he was also less than thrilled to be paired with me.

After a few songs, Luis and I retired to an empty booth. He flagged a waitress to order us a couple of drinks.

"Sorry if I seem a little off. I, uh, just got back a month or so ago."

"Well, I can understand how this might be overwhelming." I said as I considered what to say next, "Have you heard of the Walter Franks foundation?"

"A couple of buddies were talking about it, but I don't know much."

"Well, today is your lucky day."

I spent the next hour filling him in and answering his questions.

"Wow, what luck I ran into you?" He smiled, and his body relaxed for the first time. "This gives me a little hope that there is life out there for me."

"I'm glad to hear it. That's the goal of the Foundation."

"Let me make it up to you... for being a bit moody." He held out his hand and dragged me out to the dance floor.

This time was entirely different for both of us. We danced and laughed. I felt good because I got to share my work with someone I could potentially help. He seemed to have a burden lifted. His posture seemed lighter and more relaxed.

Frannie and Norm moved next to us, so we all danced together, singing with the band, dancing, and chatting as a group.

A few hours later, we headed to a nearby diner. Norm and Frannie sat on one side of the booth, and Luis and I on the other. We all ordered coffee and the breakfast special.

"So Caroline, Frannie says you run the Walter Franks Foundation. Impressive. I hear it is doing some good things for our returning vets." Norm said.

"Wait? You run it? I just thought you worked there. Wow..." Luis said, "It really is my lucky day."

"Yes, and yes, sorry I didn't tell you, but I thought the information was more important than how I knew."

"Yeah, it sounds great and just what I need." He said, "I'm planning to go over there. You should come too, Norm."

"It has helped me. Counseling, job assistance." Fran said, "I cheated a bit because she hired me."

"That's true. She's one of our best." I smiled at my friend.

"Sounds good." Norm said, "Let me know when you go. I'll tag along."

Our food arrived, and after a night of dancing, we were all starving. It was delicious, and the company was wonderful. I was glad to be out and not depressed at home or work. I would have to thank Frannie later. I had even enjoyed meeting a guy. Banner night for me.

After we finished and paid, we said goodbye to the guys with a promise to see them again. They took off in one direction as Frannie and I climbed in a cab back to our apartment.

"Oh Caroline, was he not the dreamiest?" she practically swooned.

"He is. You seem perfect together."

"Okay, getting ahead of myself here... but I can see myself marrying that man one day."

"I really hope you do, Frannie. I really do."

For the next 14 blocks, she smiled, then floated out of the cab and all the way to our 4th-floor apartment.

We decided to crash in the living room so we could sit up and gossip before bed. She told me all about Norm.

"He is from Texas. Has one brother and a sister. They still live there, as do his parents." She continued to fill me in on every detail of his life, or at least it seemed like it. I listened and responded as needed.

"So, what did you think of Luis?"

"He seemed nice. Good looking, but clearly needs our counseling services."

"Yeah, Norm said he was a bit messed up from the war."

"What about Norm? What's your opinion on his mental state?"

"Honestly, he seems okay. A little tense at times but has a good sense of humor and outgoing personality."

"Do you think he is faking it?"

She paused and looked to really consider what I said.

"Maybe, but I actually get the impression he was like this before going and is just falling back into his old ways."

"Yeah, could be."

We had seen things like with some. They aren't as impacted as others, and it seems to boil down to personality in some cases. I hope Norm was what he appeared to be for my friend's sake because she was clearly smitten.

"So, do you think you'd be open to dating Luis?"

"Oh, Fran, you know I'm not ready for that yet."

"But are you open to the idea?"

I thought about her question. I guess she's right. There is a difference between being open and being ready. Even if I didn't feel ready, could I be open enough to try?

"I honestly don't know."

I yawned and pulled the blanket around me tighter. We were quiet; the only sound was from the city outside. There were cars on the street and people talking, yelling, and laughing as they walked along the road below us.

Each time I went home to Virginia, I found it difficult to sleep in the near quiet of my roll-up the sidewalks at night hometown. But, since my parents moved a few years back, going home meant something much different now. I didn't recharge any longer in my childhood bedroom but in their new, smaller home close to downtown.

"Caroline?"

"Yeah?"

"I'm so glad we're friends."

"Me too, Fran."

Chapter Eighteen: July 1972

It was so fun to watch my friend be so in love. Fran and Norm were attached at the hip from that night forward.

She was kind-hearted, thoughtful, and had a big heart. Norm was a good guy with a big personality who filled the room with his warm spirit. They were a good pair and a great couple.

Luis and I had not made a love connection that night. Neither of us seemed in a place emotionally to connect to another person, or at least I know that was my reason.

However, Luis did come into the Foundation and had started counseling, both in our group sessions and individual appointments.

After one of his appointments, he stopped into my office to say hi.

"Knock, knock." He said at my door.

"Oh, hey, come in." I put down my pen and smiled up at him. "You had a session?"

"Yeah, it went well, I think."

"Good. I'm glad to hear it."

"Thanks. I feel more confident and relaxed already. Not as many nightmares."

"A common complaint. The nightmares, I mean." I smiled, "How is the job search going?"

"I've got an interview tomorrow. Restaurant manager."

"Oh, that's what you've been looking for. Good luck!"

"Thanks. I couldn't have done any of this without your help." He paused, "I'm so glad I met you."

I smiled but didn't reply.

"So, I was wondering," He paused, "I was wondering would you like to go to dinner tonight ... with me, if you're not busy, that is."

"Oh, hm, yeah, yes. I would love that." Wait? Did I love the idea of going out with him? It was an automatic response, and I didn't want to insult him or hurt his feelings.

"Great. I'll pick you up at 7?"

"Sounds good."

After he left, I got back to work, only to be interrupted moments later by an excited Frannie.

"Soo, what was Luis doing here?" She said, taking a seat in my guest chair.

"He was thanking me for introducing him to this place and updating me on his counseling." I knew what she wanted to hear, but I wasn't even sure I was ready to admit that I'd agreed to a date. Was it a date?

"Was that all?" She pouted.

"No." But I kept working or trying to.

"I knew it." She sat forward, "He asked you out, didn't he?"

"Yes." I finally put my pen down to look at her, "Oh, Fran, am I ready to date someone?"

"Yes, definitely, plus it's only a date, right? He didn't ask you to marry him or anything. So just what, dinner?"

"Yeah, just dinner." I sighed.

"It's been years." She took my hand, "I know it was painful, and still is for you at times, but you need to move forward. You are still alive and should live as if you are."

That made sense. I needed to allow myself to live and be alive.

I sighed, "You're right. You *are* right."

"So, you'll go?"

"Well, I was already going to go, but yes, I'm going and with a smile." I flashed a goofy smile, and she returned it with a silly one of her own. She really was the best friend. "Now you have to help me figure out what to wear!"

"Deal!"

We both left work early so I could get all dolled up for my first date in years.

"How about this?" I held up a long dress with a hot pink top and a paisley pink and green skirt. I hadn't worn this one yet, and I was dying to. It was such a fun outfit and fit me perfectly.

"What about the cream blouse with the beige plaid skirt?"

"You don't think that looks like a work outfit? I was going for hip." I looked at the hot pink and green pattern, "It seems more youthful, no?"

She studied both outfits and then flipped through my closet.

"Ya know, you were the one that worked at a fashion magazine. I mostly wear what's comfortable and fits over these hips."

"Let me try it on, and you'll see." I slipped out of my work clothes and then into the dress. The fabric was lightweight enough, and with the heat, we were having, it should be breathable.

There had been a few deaths related to the recent heat, so most people were going out early morning or late evening to avoid it. So, between the lightweight fabric and the later hour, I should be comfortable for the date.

I paired the dress with silver sandals, a few silver bangles, and a thin silver necklace. Then, I turned to model for Frannie.

"Oh, Caroline, that *is* perfect." She clasped her hands together.

"I'm glad you like it." I smiled and then twirled the skirt a bit, "I love this color, and I have the perfect new make-up."

I headed for my vanity and grabbed the new mint green eyeshadow; I applied it and then added a bit of mascara and lip gloss.

"And, done."

"I'm so excited for you. Even if there isn't a second date, I'm so proud of you for taking this step."

"Honestly, me too." I honestly meant it.

I initially was nervous and hesitant, but now that I was dressed, I was looking forward to it. He was a nice man and handsome with his short-cut dark hair and dark eyes. He was taller than me, and I was nearly six feet tall, so it wasn't often I could find a guy taller than me. We were either the same height, or the guy would be a bit shorter. But Walter had been taller. I loved it.

"Well, I'm going to get out of the way. I'm meeting Norm anyway."

"Thank you for your help." Then, I hugged her, "Wish me luck."

"Oh, dear, you won't need it. You are amazing, and what I know of Luis, he is as well." She winked, grabbed her pocketbook, and gave a two-finger wave as she went out the door.

As I waited for Luis to arrive, I paced and checked my hair, paced, and checked my make-up, paced, and checked my outfit. But, of course, I was being silly; it was just dinner out with a guy I knew, at least casually.

There was a knock on my door. I took a deep breath.

"I got this," I whispered to myself. Then, opening the door, "Hi, Luis."

"Hi, Caroline, you look ... Wow ... amazing." He smiled, looking me up and down, then leaned over to kiss my cheek, "Ready?"

"Yes." I could feel my cheeks warm. It wasn't a bad feeling.

We headed down, he flagged a cab, and we were on our way. We made small talk as we rode to the restaurant. We were going to a new Puerto Rico restaurant that had recently opened.

"I've heard good things about this place," I said.

"I went once. Reminds me of home."

"Do you miss it?"

"Sometimes, but I'm sure I'll visit soon." He gestured out the window, "I like New York better, but there is just something about your mamá's food. She made the best carne frita con cebolla."

He told me about her and his siblings, who were all still there. He hoped to get them moved here someday. The area they lived in was poor, especially after the most recent tropical storms ripped through there and left devastation behind them.

"I'll feel better once they are here."

"I'm sure."

We arrived at the restaurant and got seated near the window. I asked him to order for me as he was more familiar with the food.

"Anything you don't like?"

"Not really. I'm willing to try anything at least once."

"Alright, I'll handle it." He smiled, "You're brave to let me pick."

"I trust your judgment." I smiled back. We held our gaze for a second before the waitress came over to greet us, breaking the moment. She took our order. Luis ordered in Spanish, and I just watched him in awe. Most of the time, he had only a slight accent, but speaking Spanish, he sounded so sexy.

After the waiter left, I was looking at him all goo-goo-eyed.

"What?"

"I just hadn't heard you speak Spanish before. It sounded hot." I giggled lightly.

"Really?" He took my hand, then said something in Spanish, and my toes curled a bit.

"What's that mean?"

"I'm hungry, and here come our drinks."

"Oh." We laughed as the waitress came back to the table.

We enjoyed light conversation as we waited for our food. Laughing together, sharing stories about our lives, and just enjoying the companionship.

Our food arrived. Everything looked so good and tasted better. The mix of garlic and other spices was heavenly.

"What is this one called again?"

"Mofongo."

"Ah, it's amazing. Crisp and garlicky."

We finished up our meal. I had enjoyed every bit of it.

But my biggest surprise of the evening was how smoothly things were going and how at ease I was with him. This was definitely different than I had expected. I felt myself actually be in the moment with him and could picture myself dating for the first time.

He was funny, interesting, and had a friendly smile. He loved his family and shared stories about them.

"And my baby brother, Pedro, he is such a cut-up. Always pranking. This one time, I thought my mama was going to beat his ass. He jumped from the roof right in front of her when she was going out of the house. Scared her half to death. She chased him for two blocks swinging her chancla as she cursed him."

"Chancla?"

"Oh, yes, hm, like a flip-flop in English."

"Ah, that's funny. I can imagine."

"He is a real cut-up." He laughed, "Ready to get out of here?"

"Yes."

We left the restaurant and walked a few blocks to a piano bar. Finding a corner table, we ordered a couple of drinks. The sound was smooth as the piano notes floated around. The music was a perfect backdrop to my mood.

"I'm glad you agreed to go out with me." He said.

"I'm glad you asked."

"Me too." He set his hand on my thigh, "I honestly didn't know if you would say yes. I know you've had pain and loss."

I felt his mood shift and looked up at his face. His eyes were glassy with tears. Instinctively, I reached up and wiped a lone tear away from his cheek. He smiled weakly.

"I've had loss too." He whispered, "So I understand. Though mine is different, still it's grief."

Without thinking, I leaned forward and kissed him softly on the lips. He pulled me closer as the kiss deepened. When it ended, we looked at each other and nervously laughed.

"I'm sorry. Not sure what came over me." I said.

"I'm not sorry. I wasn't brave enough, so glad you did." He took my hand, "Ready to go?"

"Yes," I said breathlessly.

In the cab on the way back to my apartment, I felt both guilty and free. Of course, those two things shouldn't go together, but somehow that was how I felt.

"Can you wait for me?" He asked the driver, and then he held his hand out, helping me out of the cab, "I'm just going to walk her up. Two minutes max."

The driver agreed, and so we walked up to my apartment.

"Can I see you again?"

"Yes, I'd like that."

A kiss good-night or maybe two.

"Goodnight, Caroline."

"Goodnight, Luis."

It was a sweet and perfect end to my first date. I went into my apartment and straight to the window. I watched for Luis to come out of the building. When he did, my knees turned to jelly. He was handsome, and he kissed amazingly.

He looked once up at my building, but thankfully I was standing back far enough he shouldn't be able to see me. He then climbed in the cab and was gone. I watched the car as long as I could see it, and then I giggled as I went to change for bed.

Chapter Nineteen: July 1973

It had been a year now since Luis, and I started dating. Things had been going so well and that I rarely thought about Walter. The guilt had subsided, though I hadn't fully committed my heart to him yet.

Despite that, we were headed to visit my parents in Virginia. My mother was over the moon happy that I was dating someone and couldn't wait to meet him. She asked me questions every time I talked to her. Her favorite was when we were getting married.

"Mother, I have only known him a few months. I am not even close to ready for marriage, and neither is he. We haven't even said I love you yet."

"Caroline, darling, you are so stubborn. You have been with him for a year now. You're going to be an old maid, and I will not have any grandchildren."

"Mother, you have grandchildren. Denise Anne and Billy." Denise, of course, is my oldest brother, Larry's daughter was born just months before I lost Andrew and Billy, who was my brother, Karl's son. "Plus, Larry and Mary Jane will have a second child any day now."

I never said it, but I wanted to remind her she also had Andrew, even if briefly. I know that she never saw him, never felt him, held him. He wasn't real to her, but he was real to me. He was still in my heart, and I would never forget him, ever.

She was right about one thing; we had been together for a year, and in all the time, we hadn't said I love you to each other. I think he knew that I was still broken and didn't pressure me. He carried his own scars and baggage and was still seeing a counselor with the Foundation to discuss his experiences in Vietnam, so I know he was just as broken as I was.

It caused Luis anxiety to be in a confined space, like an airplane, so we borrowed a car. Then, if he got anxious, we could pull over for him to relax. Thankfully, we only had to do it twice on the drive down.

I held his hand as he focused on his breathing. The second time he recovered much quicker than the first.

As we neared my parents' home, I apologized in advance for anything that might be said by my mother.

"No need to apologize. I am really good with parents." He winked. It was just a simple gesture, but it eased some of my anxiety, and I felt my body relax.

As predicted, my mother was embarrassingly excited. She gushed over him from the moment we stepped in the door, asking questions faster than Luis could answer. She either didn't care or didn't notice because she just kept going.

"Oh, Luis, it is so nice to finally meet you. Did you have a nice drive down?"

"Thank you, yes it was-"

"So, tell us about yourself! Where are you from? What do you do? So, you were in Vietnam? How long were you there? And when are you going to marry Caroline?"

"Mother! Oh, my goodness... I'm sorry, Luis."

"No apology necessary. I get it. Mrs. Graham, I love Caroline, but we aren't quite ready. We both have grief we carry with us. So for now, we just enjoy living in sin." He winked at me and gave my hand a squeeze. My heart swelled because the look he left on my mother's face was priceless.

She sat down stunned. Not to mention he said he loved me. At that moment, I knew I loved him too but would have to wait until later to tell him.

My dad stepped forward at that point, "How 'bout a beer, Luis?"

"Yes, sir. I'd love one."

He took Luis out to the garage to talk man stuff. I just watched him go and then turned to my mother.

"How could you ask him that? I have already told you we weren't ready. We hadn't even said I love yous yet."

"Yes, but it seems he has said he loves you now. I have to go check on dinner." She smirked as she left the room, clearly recovered from any shock, real or fake, she might have had moments ago. Had that been her plan all along?

In truth, we hadn't slept together yet, keeping things to kissing, and that was all. Until now, neither of us seemed ready to take our relationship to that level.

My parents' new house had two guest bedrooms in addition to their room. I had asked if we could sleep in separate rooms, and as we weren't serious, it seemed like the best choice. My mother hadn't batted an eye at the request and fixed up both rooms for us.

I can't believe I was the same person who took off with her boyfriend just a few years ago to live in New York City. Now I was taking things nice and slow. I had been younger, naïve. Plus, there had been an almost instant connection with Walter. I knew from almost day one that he was my person.

With Luis, I hadn't had that spark. Though I could feel the shift in our relationship each day as we got to know each other better.

The evening went well. My brothers Larry and Karl came with their wives and children. Denise Anne will be 5 soon. She was talkative and followed me everywhere, asking me questions about New York City. Billy was 2 years old and rambunctious. He ran around and climbed on anything and anyone he could. Larry and Mary Jane's second baby would be born at any moment.

It was a bit bittersweet to watch the children and see her pregnant. But I shook off my bad feelings and focused on something happy, like having another nephew or niece soon.

"Oh, Mary Jane, your belly is so cute," I said as I sat next to her.

"Thanks. I feel big as a house."

"I'm sure."

We chatted and soon Jan, my brother Karl's wife, came to join us. Unfortunately, I didn't know them as well as I would like. We talked at family events, but not much outside of that.

"We should talk more," I said during a lull in the conversation.

"We really should." Mary Jane agreed.

"I'm not sure why we don't," Jan added.

"Well, I say we start a weekly phone call, so we stay in touch. You both have my telephone and address, and I have yours."

We all agreed to it.

When dinner was done, and my brothers and their families were leaving, Larry leaned over to hug me.

"Luis is good people, Caroline. I hope you're happy."

I looked up at my oldest brother, "I am."

It was odd how good it felt to admit that. This whole trip had been a blessing for our relationship. It really shined a light on what a great, amazing man Luis was. Patient, friendly with a good sense of humor. He fit right in with my family well. My father had been engaged in heavy conversation with Luis most of the night. It was amazing.

So later that night, as everyone slept, I crept down the hall to the guest room Luis was sleeping in. I took a deep breath so I didn't lose my nerve. Softly I knocked on the door as I pushed it open.

"Luis?"

"Caroline? Is everything okay?"

"Yes... I ... yes, everything is fine." I slowly slipped my shoulders out of my nightgown, letting it fall into a puddle of satin and lace to the floor.

He inhaled slightly. "Oh Caroline, you are so beautiful. Come here, my love." He lifted the sheets to allow me to lie next to him. We kissed with a sweet but intense passion.

Neither of us had made love for several years. Our bodies reacted with instinct at the touch and the awakening inside. As we kissed and touched, the need for each other grew and grew until we couldn't wait any longer.

"I love you, Luis," I whispered.

"I love you too, Caroline."

The rest of our visit was fairly uneventful. Though my mother continued her barrage of questioning, and my father offered an out to Luis any chance he could.

Luis and I were thrilled with the change in our relationship. It had been the right time to take things to the next level. I couldn't wait to get back to New York to explore our new relationship further.

Chapter Twenty: November 1973

I was working in my office, having skipped lunch, again. A bad habit of mine when I was working. Today I was interviewing new counselors, leaving little time for myself. The foundation had gotten so popular that we needed to fill 6 more positions for counselors, plus I needed 8 more job placement specialists.

I was making notes about my last interview when Frannie came in.

"I'm sure you skipped lunch again." She plopped a brown paper bag on my desk.

"You know me too well."

But I didn't look up right away. When I did, I realized she was holding her hand in a funny position and had the biggest grin on her face.

"Wait? Did he –?"

"He did!" She squealed, "Just now at lunch."

"Oh, Fran!" I jumped up and hugged her, grasping her hand to examine the ring closer, "It's gorgeous."

"Thank you. I think so." She looked down at her ring.

"I need details, how? When?" I pulled her to the small couch in my office.

"We were at lunch, and he suggested we go for a short walk over to Central Park." She giggled.

"But it's cold out."

"Yeah, but I didn't notice." She sighed. "We just walked from the south entrance around a bit. He stopped me at a bench so he could tie his shoe. I wasn't really watching him, but he was taking a long time, so I looked back, and he was on one knee with a ring in hand. A small crowd started to form, and they gasped and chanted for us. Not that I would have, but how could I say no!"

"I'm so happy for you. For you both."

"Thanks." She giggled again.

"I guess we have to start planning a wedding!"

We spent the next several months planning their wedding. It was a small event with less than 60 people, but I wanted it to be perfect for my best friend. She deserved so much happiness.

The first order of business was to find a venue. They wanted to get married in New York even though Norm's family lived in Texas. They were happy to travel for him.

On the other hand, Frannie had a much smaller family with just her mother, a sister, and an aunt. They lived in New Jersey, so no travel was needed, just a quick ride over the George Washington bridge.

It took us a few weeks, but we found a small chapel with a reception area that we could rent for a Friday afternoon and into the evening.

"This will be perfect. With the chapel and then reception area so close. Plus, it has those rooms we can use to dress ahead of time." Frannie said.

"I agree. This will easily hold your guests plus have space to breathe a bit." I said, looking around mentally, counting seats. "Looks like ten on each of these two sides and then ten rows."

"We won't have nearly that many people, though."

"Oh, I know. But, you know me, just like to know what we are working with."

We left the chapel area and went back to the reception space. The church already had tables with chairs set out.

"I like these rounds tables." Fran said, "Are these staying?"

We both looked at the church secretary.

"Oh, yes, we can take some out if you don't need this many."

I did another count. "Looks like this is for 200?"

"That's right."

"Oh, we only have 58 people on the list." Frannie looked around, "This is a huge space."

"Well, just think of how much room we'll have for dancing." I offered with a laugh.

"You have a point there."

After the tour was complete, we followed the secretary to the office to complete the contract and give the deposit.

"You're all set. We will see you in April." She pushed a copy of the contract across the desk.

"Thank you so much," Frannie said.

Back on the street, we decided to grab lunch and talk about the next steps. So we headed a few blocks south and into a deli. We ordered a couple of pastrami sandwiches with extra pickles.

We found a table overlooking the street.

"I'm so glad we found that place. It is perfect!" Frannie said, "Next up, wedding dress."

"Yes, and I already have a few ideas I want to show you."

"I'm so glad. I have no idea where to start." She smiled, "I'm so glad I met you for so many reasons."

"Me too."

We ate and chatted, mostly about her wedding, but a little about work. Things were busy but good. We were helping a lot of people.

I had started to sit in on a few of the spouse support sessions. I had framed it to the counselors as I was observing for performance and improvement opportunities, but the truth was, I loved hearing others' experiences. It made me feel more normal, and that still feeling grief, though it was less lately, was okay.

"It is has been nearly five years since I lost Harold. I think about him every single day." One wife said, "I just look at our daughter and see him in her smile. I grief for the other children we will never have."

"Yes, I don't think I will ever get over my boyfriend's death." Another lady shared, "We had big plans for our future."

I related to these ladies so much, but I sat quietly in a corner, sticking with my lie about being here to observe. Still, listening was helpful, and I didn't feel strange.

Being here with Fran, planning her wedding when I never got to do this, brought up all kinds of feelings in me. Anger, regret, sadness, but also happiness. I didn't resent or envy her happiness, just upset at losing mine.

"Do you have thoughts on what we should serve at the wedding?" Fran asked, bringing me back to our conversation.

"Do you want a sit-down dinner or a buffet?"

"I'm thinking buffet. Less formal and we can have a variety. Nobody is stuck with just one food choice."

"I like that idea."

"Luis manages at that new steakhouse; it might be a good choice." She said.

"Yeah, they have good food. He might even be able to work out a good price for you." I'd eaten there a few times; it was good food.

"That would be nice, but I hate to take advantage of him." She said, "We have some money saved, but I would prefer not to spend it all on our wedding."

"In that case, I have a crazy idea about your wedding dress. Want to hear it?"

"Definitely."

"Well, I already talked to her, actually she offered, but my mother said she could make it for you."

"Are you serious?" Fran grabbed my hand, "I would love for her to make it. She is a beautiful seamstress."

It was true. My mother had been commissioned by many ladies back home to make them dresses. She had made most of mine growing up, and she is one reason I knew so much about fashion.

"She's pretty excited about it and said she can come to visit us soon to get started. She's going to mail you some pictures with her ideas."

"Your mother is a lifesaver. Mine can't even reattach a button, but she can mix a good drink."

Frannie's mother had worked in a bar in one capacity or another all of Frannie's life. She had even worked in speakeasies during the Prohibition years. The stories she told of that time could fill a book and make a grown man blush.

"That just leaves flowers and decor, really. Oh, and of course, bridesmaids." I said.

"Obviously, you're my maid of honor.... But I think that's it. We are just having you and Luis stand up with us. No others."

"Not even your sister. What about his brother and sister? Will they be involved?"

"No, with them traveling, we discussed it. It will be easier to not give them duties. My sister and I aren't that close, as you know, so no, just you and Luis."

"Well, that's easy enough. The men get suits, and my mom can make our dresses."

"And we can do white daisies with red roses." She said.
"Perfect. Wedding planning under control."

Chapter Twenty-One: April 1974

The big day arrived. The day was gorgeous. Blue sky and sunshine, not a cloud in the sky. Frannie was giddy with excitement. I knew she was going to have a happy life with Norm. There were no two people better matched than Norm and Frannie. His strengths were her weaknesses, and her strengths were his weaknesses. It was the perfect balance of yin and yang.

Once Frannie was dressed, her hair done, and make-up applied, she turned to face me. Her dress was a cream-colored tea-length gown with a petticoat and white lace overlay. Once again, my mother had outdone herself with this creation. It perfectly fits Frannie's personality with just the right amount of sparkle but not overstated.

My dress was also tea-length but without the petticoat under. It was a pale pink satin with a cream lace overlay. I handed her the daisy and rose bouquet.

"Frannie, you look simply stunning."

"Thank you ... Oh, Caroline, this is really happening!" she turned back towards her reflection, "I am about to become Mrs. Norman Michael Dailey."

At that moment, there was a knock on the door. We were using one of the church classrooms as a dressing area. We had brought in a floor-length mirror and a small room divider from our apartment. The room divider was so we could change behind it without flashing anyone that might open the door.

"Come in," I said.

It was our mothers and also Norm's mother.

"Oh, Frannie, you're gorgeous." Her mother, Essie, said, "You did a wonderful job on the dress, Connie. It fits her flawlessly." Essie had Fran turn to show it all.

"She was a fun bride to work with." My mother smiled.

Fran hugged her and then looked at her soon-to-be mother-in-law, Alice. She was quietly watching, but then I noticed her eyes were watery.

"I couldn't ask for a more beautiful person, inside and out for my Norman." Alice finally said, her voice cracking. She dabbed at her eyes.

"Thank you. I am so happy and blessed to be with him as well."

There was again a knock on the door. It was Fran's sister Ginger.

"Ready, sis?"

Frannie took a deep breath and nodded. Then, everyone filed out, returning to their seats, leaving just to the two of us. I touched up her make-up, fluffed her dress.

"Okay, ready?" I asked.

"Yeah."

We hugged and then walked down the hall to await her cue. Unfortunately, she had no father to walk her, so she asked me to lead her down the aisle. Her reason made me laugh.

"We both got to get there somehow; why not together?"

So now we stood there waiting for our cue.

"I'm so very happy for you, Fran."

"Thanks, Caroline, for everything."

When the music changed, we linked arms and began our walk. My friend to her groom and me to support her. Thankfully, thoughts of Walter hadn't clouded my memory today. Instead, I was able to simply focus on my friends.

Norm wiped at his eyes when he saw Frannie walking down the aisle towards him. Even Luis had a few tears in his eyes, but his smile was aimed at me.

They had written their own vows, and Norm's, as usual, was funny. Full of inside jokes as well as heartfelt sentiments.

The reception area was decorated simply with white tablecloths on each table with a simple glass vase with white daisies and red roses. There were also bright balloons in white and red with long curl ribbons hung around the room.

Luis's restaurant had provided catering for us, plus he brought in a few servers to assist. They even had an excellent pastry chef who made the cake. It was a 3-layer lemon cream cake.

There was a small band from their favorite club, and aside from the venue, the band had been the next most expensive wedding item. They would start to play after most people had eaten. But, for now, they were standing in line for food and chatting with the other guests.

Fran and Norm came in several minutes later. They had gone to one of the dressing rooms to savor their first few moments as a married couple. Upon entering, the crowd cheered, and the room filled with congratulations and well wishes. They were encouraged to go to the front of the buffet line.

As they made their way along, they shook hands, thanked people, and gave hugs to guests they were only just seeing. I wiped a tear as I watched my friend glow with pure joy. Her smile filled the room, and I could hear her voice and laughter above all others.

Luis came to stand next to me, "You look beautiful, Caroline." He whispered, "I know today is supposed to be about them, but I couldn't take my eyes off of you."

"Is that why you almost fumbled the ring?" I teased.

"That was embarrassing. Thank goodness Norm has good reflexes."

We made our way through the buffet line and then to join the newlyweds at the head table. I looked around as I sat down. The wedding was perfect, but I couldn't help at that moment to let my mind wander. Would I ever have this? Did I want this?

I glanced to my right. Luis was such a sweet and handsome guy, but could I picture myself with him? Thankfully I didn't have to worry about that yet. We weren't there.

I smiled at him when he caught me looking at him and then focused on my food. I could feel his eyes on me, so I shifted uncomfortably in my seat.

"Oh, this roast is superb." I said to him to break up the tense moment, "Give my compliments to your chef."

"He did a great job."

With dinner nearly wrapped up, the band took the stage, starting with a few jazz numbers to set the mood. Norm and Fran headed out for their first dance. I watched my friend smiling up at her new husband.

"They look so good together," I whispered.

"They do," Luis said.

As their first dance ended, the band invited everyone to join them on the dance floor.

"Care to dance, Ms. Caroline," Luis said, extending his hand out.

"Don't mind if I do." I dropped my napkin into my chair as I stood, taking his hand.

He led me to the dance floor and then guided me expertly all around it. I always enjoyed dancing with Luis. He was smooth and graceful.

As we danced, Luis whispered, "We should get married."

I felt a wave of panic shoot through my whole body and an alarm sound deep in my soul. No, he must be joking. Yes, that must be it. He is joking.

"Ha, ha. Yes, we must. Tomorrow."

"No, Caroline. I'm serious." He stopped dancing, "I love you and want to spend the rest of my life with you."

The hope in his eyes told me what I feared most – he was serious. Hadn't I just been thinking about this? I thought I would have more time before making any decisions. I loved him, but I wasn't in love with him, at least not enough to take this step with him, not like I was with Walter. I really hoped I would be.

"Oh, hm... Luis, I... you *are* serious. I'm sorry." I stumbled on my words, "I don't think this is the right time for this? It's our best friends' wedding, and the focus should be on them, don't you think?"

My whole heart was screaming on the inside. Not only did I not want to take the focus off of Norm and Frannie, but I also didn't want to have to break his heart. Not tonight.

"No, no, you are right." He looked around, and his eyes found Norm and Frannie dancing happily just a few couples away from us. His eyes softened, "Bad timing. It should be about them today."

He took me in his arms again, and we started dancing, but I could tell he was crushed by the way his laugh wasn't as deep and his posture soft, not as confident. Almost like the first day I met him.

I had worried about this day for so long. I wanted to love him like I loved Walter. I wanted to marry him in my head, but in my heart was a completely different story.

"I love you, Caroline." He whispered as we danced, "We can talk about it later, perhaps?"

"Yes, let's table it for now." I tried to smile a happy, loving smile, but his pinched face told me it hadn't translated that way to him.

The rest of the reception was a blur. I dreaded the time when we would be alone. I wasn't ready to answer that question.

Looking at my friends, they seemed so happy. I wanted to be like them, and I wanted that for Luis as well.

I wondered could I marry him and live the rest of my life knowing in my heart that I didn't fully love him. Was that even fair? Luckily, I didn't have to decide that night. Instead, we focused on our friends and nothing more.

Chapter Twenty-Two: August 1974

It was actually several months before I had to face the dreaded question. I had my guard up for months waiting. I lost countless nights of sleep worrying. Then just when I started to relax and let my guard up, he brought it up again.

We had a wonderful dinner out at a new restaurant and had gone back to my apartment. I was fixing us a nightcap when I turned to see him down on one knee, ring in hand.

"Caroline, I didn't know I could love someone as much as I love you. You restored my faith and made me believe in life again. I was so lost after the war, but your smile made each day worth getting up for. Please give me the honor of making you that happy for the rest of our lives."

"Oh... oh Luis... I don't know what to say."

"Please say yes." He said softly.

"I can't. I can't say yes today. I'm just not ready. Please don't ask me tonight."

"Are you serious? You brushed me off at the wedding, and so I waited. I knew I scared you then, but it has been months." He pushed himself up with a huff, "I thought I should give you time to get used to the idea. What more can I do?"

"You can't do anything." I sighed, "This is about me and what I lost. I have tried, Luis. I want to want this, but I just feel too broken."

"Walter? Are you talking about your dead fiancée that you lost years ago?"

"Yes," I barely said it above a whisper because I knew it was silly.

Walter had been gone for five years now, and I knew he wasn't coming back and that he would want me to move on. But someone hadn't told my heart that it was time to move on, to heal, and to let go.

"It is normal and natural for people to seek a companion and partner in life. You need to learn to live without him. You need to accept he is not coming back and learn to move on with your life. If you don't, you will be alone forever. I love you. I love you now, and I am here in front of you asking you to marry me, spend the rest of our lives together. Walter is gone, but I am here." He paused and looked at me. His eyes searched my face, "So, what do you want, Caroline? A ghost or a man on his knees begging to love you for the rest of his life?"

"Luis, I... I just can't. I love you; I do, but the love I have for ... and the pain too. It still feels so fresh to me." Tears streamed down my face, "I'm so sorry."

I wanted to say so many other things. Like how I wanted to continue our relationship as we were now. In time, I could love him like that, right?

He just nodded and picked up his jacket off the couch. He turned to look at me and appeared like he might say something but instead walked out of the door and my life forever.

I stood unmoving for what felt like an eternity until the pain in my heart brought me to my knees. I collapsed to the floor in a puddle of tears. What was left of my heart was shattered.

This break-up pushed me over the cliff I didn't realize I was standing on. I cried almost non-stop for days. I cried for Luis. I cried for Walter. I cried for sweet little Andrew.

I cried more, though, for myself. Luis was right. I needed to learn to be happy alone and give up on a ghost.

"Oh, Walter," I said out loud, "I miss you so much. I feel like I failed you, us, Andrew. Being careless, I killed our little boy. The proof of our love, and I was so careless with him." I shook with sorrow as I continued my weeping monologue to the heavens. "I should have married you before you left. Maybe then things would have been different. Maybe then Andrew would have lived. Maybe you would have lived. I was stupid, selfish, and naive to think otherwise."

I punched hard at my pillow several times. I put all my anger, frustration, and sadness into those punches. I wanted this grief to be gone. I held the pillow to my mouth, screaming.

This is what I needed to do. Get all this out, all the pain, and all the years of holding it in. I was never going to move on with life unless I dealt with it. Something we told all the veterans coming through the door, but I had focused for years on them but never focused on myself.

As exhaustion started to take hold of me, I rolled to my back.

"I know I must accept you are gone. I must move on with my life and learn who I am without you. I thought I was doing it, but clearly, I was faking it. I will always love you, but I need to set myself free ... Goodbye, my love. Rest well until we meet again."

I continued to cry until I fell into a dreamless sleep. I slept for twelve straight hours. When I woke, I felt lighter and more alive than I had in years. My head hurt, and my face was puffy from crying, but I could feel the relief instantly.

After that night, I threw myself into work. I took on more responsibility and stopped delegating things to my secretary and other team members. Besides, I liked to have my hands in all the processes and goings-on. It felt like important work and that we were helping people.

I continued to sit in on many of the family counseling sessions. It was helpful for me, especially with this break-up.

"So Caroline, you join us a lot. Would you like to share anything?" Nancy, the counselor she knew the origins of the Walter Franks Foundation to a point, but not my connection to Walter Franks.

"Hm, no, I couldn't. I'm just here to observe." I lifted my pad of paper and pen.

"You don't know anyone important to you that was lost there?"

My breathing quickened, and I felt my stomach twist. I exhaled.

"Yeah, there was someone." I heard myself say, "Walter Franks."

Everyone in the room gasped and began whispering to their neighbor.

"Would you like to share about Walter?" Nancy asked, not showing a sign that she was surprised or shocked. Perhaps she knew more than I thought she did.

I took a deep breath, looked around the room without truly seeing anyone, and then shared about him.

"And then I lost the baby. He lived for only a few days before passing. I was home recovering when I found out about Walter's death."

"That was, you said, 5 years ago?" Nancy asked.

"Yes."

"Did you seek counseling then?"

"No, this is the first time, and I'm just here observing."

"You have been observing the group for a while now, several months," Nancy said, "Are you sure it's just observing?"

I gaped at her. She had called me out, though she wasn't wrong. I might have come originally to observe for work, but I found that hearing the other's stories helped my loneliness. I wasn't the only heartbroken not-quite widow in the world. There were three in this group alone.

"No, you're right. You *are* so right. That's why you are our best." I smiled at her and then the group of ladies, "It did start as observation, but I realized that ... I realized that I could probably benefit from this group."

"I'm so glad you shared with us, and you should continue to join us, and not just to observe." Nancy winked, "Okay, who's next?"

After the session, I had several of the ladies hug me and let me know they were glad I shared and to keep in touch.

"Thanks, Nancy. I'm glad you called on me."

"Oh, I am so glad you finally shared, even if it was at my nudging." She hugged me, "Please, please come again. Anytime."

"You know, I think I will." I smiled brightly and bounced away, feeling lighter than I had in a long time.

I decided I deserved to go out for lunch. As Fran was off today, I headed out by myself. What did I want to eat? So many choices.

I walked randomly and, in my daydreaming, I hadn't noticed a familiar face walking towards me.

"Caroline Graham, is that you?" It was Betty from Groove.

"Oh, Betty, hi." I smiled and then noticed her large round belly and bright-eyed toddler in tow.

"It has been a long time." She rubbed her belly and then gestured to her toddler, "This is Grant and this one; well, I'm not sure who this little one will be, but they are due any day now. And what about you? Any children?"

"No, not yet, but congratulations to you. Grant is previous." I smiled down at the child. He looked at me and started barking. "Oh my."

"Grant, stop that." She scolded, "We are going through a doggy phase."

"Ah, well, cute."

"So, whatever happened to you? I know you left Groove after ... oh I'm sorry, I remember now." Her tone actually sounded sincere.

"Yes, well, it was good to see you. Congratulations again." I quickly walked away, not wanting to reminisce any longer with my once enemy. Enemy was a strong word, more like a mean girl.

I walked for a couple of blocks before deciding to just head back to the office without lunch and feeling like my recovery just took two steps back.

Why did I have to see her today of all days? Why did she get everything that I wanted? She wasn't a nice person, but I was. Didn't I deserve those things?

The universe didn't answer me, and I didn't expect to find it on the streets of New York, so I threw myself back into my work. It was the only thing in my life that gave me true pleasure.

Chapter Twenty-Three: October 1974

"Knock, knock," Frannie said at my office door.

"Oh, come in."

"Monthly call with Mr. Butler?"

I had just ended a call with him. He was our chairman of the board, and I was the co-chair and president of our Foundation after giving him the monthly updates on the foundation's finances, our veteran reach, and updates on our staffing. I finally felt like the company was in a good position with the number of employees.

We would be presenting to the entire board in a week.

"Yep. It went well. He's happy with things."

"Good. He should. Things are going well."

"They are."

"So, I wanted to talk to you about something." She paused and looked at her lap.

"What's going on? Everything okay?"

"Yes, yes, but Norman was offered a job." She said, still looking at her lap.

"Oh?" That sounded like good news, but her tone didn't make it sound good.

"Yeah, but it's in ... Texas."

"Oh, I see." I stood and went to sit in the chair next to her, "Are you happy about it?"

"I am, but I'm worried about you."

"Me? Why?"

"Because you don't do anything but work and only go out if I force you, which obviously hasn't happened much since I got married and moved out." She reached for my hand, "I don't want you to be alone here."

"I'm not alone. I have –" Who did I have besides her and Norm?

There were the Butlers. However, they recently moved to upstate New York and only drove to the city a few times a year now.

I hadn't kept in touch with anyone else from Groove, though I did bump into Sally and Bert sometimes. Of course, a random encounter didn't count as a friendship.

I had bumped into Betty that one day, but she was definitely not a friend. My girlfriends from home had all moved on with their lives and were married raising children now.

I did have my sisters-in-law. As promised, we had gotten better at keeping in touch and growing our relationships, but they weren't close enough to meet for lunch or a night out. Plus, they had their hands full with their children as well.

"See? You can't name anyone, and if it wasn't for me, most days you probably wouldn't even eat."

"That ... might be true." I squeezed her hand, "But, please, Fran, don't worry about me. I'll be fine. We have telephones and letters. Plus, I can come visit you. I've never been to Texas."

She looked at me, "Are you sure you'll be alright here without me?"

I laughed, "Yes! You can't babysit me forever. You've got Norm, and you need to start your life and family."

She searched my face, tears forming in her eyes. My own were feeling watery as well. I was truly happy for my friend.

"I promise to keep in touch. I don't want to be one of those used to know people." She said.

"Of course not! We are friends for life." I checked the time, "Hey, why don't we go grab lunch?"

"I'm in."

A week later, they flew down to Houston to do some house hunting and scope out the area. They came back sharing all about a small-town just south of the city. She said it was a quaint, quiet place with friendly people.

"Oh, Caroline, it is so amazing." Frannie said as we sat in a coffee shop catching up, "We found a charming little neighborhood that is being built now. The house we picked out is perfect. It is 4 bedrooms, can you imagine? After living in these tiny apartments, I'm looking forward to a big house."

"It sounds wonderful."

Even though it was just me, I had to admit that I would love a little more space. Since Fran and Norm married, I had moved into a 400 square foot 1 bedroom apartment. I wouldn't need 4 bedrooms, but two or three would be nice.

"It is. The town is adorable. I can't wait for you to come to visit."

"I can't wait." I sipped my coffee, "Still planning to leave at the beginning of November?"

"That's the plan. We want to get out of here before the snow, plus his job starts then as well."

"Makes sense." I chuckled, "So, we only have about 2 weekends left to throw you a big going away party."

"Ha, yes, we have to, but I have so much to do before then. Maybe we can make it a packing party."

"Deal!"

We got to work making plans and a guest list for their farewell and house-packing party.

"What about Luis? Are you up for seeing him again?"

"I don't know." I hadn't seen him since he walked out of my apartment. I heard he had canceled all his remaining appointments at the Foundation, and that, above everything else, hurt me the most. I hated to be the source of his pain, "I doubt he would want to see me."

"Well, he has started to date someone new."

"He has?"

"Yes. I've met her once. She seems nice."

"Good for him."

I wanted to mean it, and I had no right to feel jealous, but I did. I wish I could move on so quickly. Even though I wasn't ready to marry him, I had loved him. Still loved him in some way.

I needed to put it out of my head and stop being selfish. He deserved to be loved the way he loved them. Unfortunately, I was not that person.

Less than a month later, I stood on the curb in front of Norm and Frannie's apartment. Their rented moving truck was nearly loaded and ready to get out on the road. Norm was bringing down the last box now, and then they'd begin their journey to their new home in Glenn Lake, Texas.

"Make sure you call me when you get there," I said.

"I will." She was clutching the handle of the goody bag I gave her. It had snacks, magazines, and new stationery, so she'd have no reason not to write me.

"Please take lots of pictures. I added extra film in that bag."

"Of course, and I'll send you the extra copies."

We stood there for a moment, not knowing what to say. Both of us fighting tears. Norm had brought the last box down and secured it into the truck.

"Oh, Fran, I'm so excited for you."

"Thanks. Now my asks of you," She winked, "Make some new friends at least a lunch buddy, and also promise to eat lunch at least once in a while."

We laughed as tears began to fall. Norm came over.

"Ready to go, darlin'?" He put his arm around her waist.

She looked at me and then grabbed me for a farewell hug.

"I will miss you so much, friend."

"I will miss you too," I said.

"Oh, y'all," Norm said as he joined in the good-bye hug.

Once we were done, they climbed into the cab of the truck. Frannie hung out the passenger window and waved until they were gone.

I stood there for several minutes, hoping they would come back, but knowing they were doing the best thing for themselves. It was a positive step for them.

For me, it was an opportunity to branch out without having that safety net friendship. I'd start with taking myself out to breakfast. I headed to my favorite diner, ordered a short stack and a side of bacon. I ate it while the sun crept up through the buildings and watched as the city woke up for the day.

After breakfast, I decided to pop into some of my favorite shops. I found a few new outfits, a new-used handbag in perfect condition, and a colored vase that would be perfectly perched on the shelf near my kitchen window. I could imagine the sun streaming through it and painting my walls in reds and greens.

With shopping finished, I started to head back to my apartment, stopping in the corner store for a sandwich. It would be my lunch and supper.

When I got into my apartment, my phone was ringing. I dropped the bags on my sofa and dove for the phone. I was expecting it to be Frannie saying they had stopped for the day, but knowing Norm would push things, I was guessing something must be wrong.

"Hello?"

"Caroline? It's mom."

"Oh, hi, mom. What's going on?" She never called me out of the blue and definitely not on a Saturday in the middle of the day. She had her quilting group on Saturdays, and we always had a set call on Wednesday evenings.

"Hm, I ... I have breast cancer." Her voice cracked.

"Oh, mom. How or what, or I don't know what to ask." My throat felt instantly dry. I sat on one of my kitchen stools.

"They said stage 3. So I'll be going to have the lumps removed and then start treatment from there."

"Do they think it has spread?"

"They don't think so, but I'll need further tests, and either way, they'll start treatments."

"Alright, well, when do your treatments start?"

"In two weeks, that's when I'm scheduled for a lumpectomy ."

"That's fast, is that fast?"

"They want to be aggressive." Her voice cracked, "I'm scared."

"I will make arrangements to come to stay with you and help you and dad out."

"Thank you."

After getting off the phone with her, I collapsed onto the couch. This was not what I had ever expected to happen, not today, not ever. Not to my mother, but here we were. I knew medical procedures had come a long way, but it was still scary.

I pulled myself together and called the airlines to arrange my travel home. This time it was to comfort my mother. The woman who had been my rock for so long.

Chapter Twenty-Four: November 1974

"Are you comfortable, mother?" I asked as I tucked her in bed.

We had brought her home from the hospital. Her surgery had gone well, and after a few days of rest and monitoring, we were able to bring her home to recover.

"As comfortable as I can be."

"You have a few hours before you can take more pain medicine, so try to rest until then." I put a handbell next to her on the nightstand, "Ring if you need something."

I headed down the hall to the kitchen. I pulled out the pill bottles and a pad of paper to make a schedule. I wanted to keep her as pain-free as possible.

My father came in from the garage and grabbed a beer from the fridge. Popping the top, he took a long drag on it, then looked at me.

"She get settled in okay?"

"She did. Now she's resting." I said.

"Good." He took another sip of beer, "Thank you for coming. I couldn't do this without you."

"Of course. I'm glad to be able to help."

He nodded and then headed back to his garage. He always had a woodworking project going on, especially since he retired last year. He sold some pieces, gave some away, and kept others.

I started sorting out the casseroles and freezer meals that neighbors, church members, and family had sent over. We would be eating these for a month. I wrote down all the names so I could send thank you cards which would be my next task.

The phone rang, so I grabbed it quickly, so it didn't wake my mother up.

"Hello?"

"Hi, Caroline, it's Larry."

"Oh, hi, Larry."

"I just wanted to check on mom. Did you get her home okay?"

"Yes, she's resting now."

"Great. Did everything go alright?"

"It did. The doctor said they won't know for sure if they got everything. She is scheduled for a scan next week, and then she'll start radiation after that."

"Well, let us know if you need anything."

"I will."

The rest of the afternoon was quiet. I got all the thank you notes written out and addressed. I'd toss them in the mail tomorrow.

Checking the clock, it was time for mother's pain medicine. As I was getting her a glass of water, I heard the bell ring from her room.

"I'm coming," I yelled out to her.

I added some soda crackers and the glass of water to a tray and then had her pills in a tiny cup for ease of carrying. Finally, I headed down the hall and pushed her door open.

"Here we are." I set the tray on her dresser and then grabbed the water and pills. "Did you sleep alright?"

"I did." She sat up and winced.

"Careful." I helped her sit up.

"Thank you."

I handed her the cup with the pills and then waited with her water.

"I also brought some crackers, in case you think you can eat a few."

"Not now, but leave them close by."

"Do you need to get up?" I asked.

"Hm, yes, I need to use the bathroom."

"I'll help you get up."

The reversal of roles was strange, but I was happy to be here for her. I thought of all the times she nursed me through an illness and how she was there for me during my grief and recovery.

I got her settled in the bathroom and then waited nearby in case she needed help. Moments later, she came to the door, and I helped her back to bed. I stayed with her until she got sleepy again.

There wasn't much else for me to do while she slept, so I grabbed a book and went to the living room. I wouldn't need to cook supper as it was handled. It would just require me to warm and serve; even my father could handle that.

Not that he was helpless, but he had depended on my mother to handle things for so long. He never tried or learned.

He was a remarkable man in so many other ways; he'd worked until his retirement and had been in World War II years before. He loved his family and had been a wonderful provider. I gave him a pass on knowing some of the basic household things.

Plus, he lived a simple life with his routine, and now his wife was ill, and it had sent his world upside down. I could tell he was worried and maybe in a slight depression, so I was here for him as much as for her.

It was now a few weeks since mother's surgery. She was doing well but her radiation had started. I had hoped to go back to New York to check in on work, but her treatment was causing her some fatigue, so I stayed.

I called the office regularly to check in with my secretary. She was a godsend and helping to hold down the fort and would be getting a nice bonus and a raise for the new year.

For now, I was needed here, and I would stay as long as possible, depending on my wonderful staff to keep the foundation going.

Currently, mother was resting, which she did a lot these days, and I was in the living room with a book, which was becoming our typical day. Meals were provided by others and warmed up.

My father, on the other hand, was a mess. He had always been a quiet man, but suddenly he wanted to talk.

Maybe it helped him process what was happening. But, I know for me, it helped the time pass as we waited. It felt like we were always waiting these days. For doctors to call. For the next checkup. For her to get well. All just waiting.

"I remember when you were about five. You got it in your head that you were going to be an acrobat in the circus. You became obsessed. It was my fault for taking you to the circus. You tumbled and jumped and made everything into a trapeze." He laughed, "It scared your mother near to death. She was always fussing at you to get down from here or stop jumping off of that."

I listened to him talk. Again, it was nice to hear, even the stories I had heard hundreds of times, but this time was from his point of view.

"Then, when you were seven, you wanted to be a veterinarian. You had found a sick bird in the yard, and you were determined to heal it. And you did. That was it. You were sure that was your calling. You looked for every sick animal you could to help. I don't know where you found them all, but you tried so hard."

The phone rang, interrupting his story. We were waiting on a call from my mother's doctor with the results of her recent scan.

"Hello." I listened while my father talked to him. His frown and lack of response told me a lot. It wasn't good news. His shoulder dropped more and more through the call. "Thank you, Doctor Brown."

I watched him as he set the phone back in the cradle. He then sat down.

"It's not good news." He mumbled.

"It's spread, hasn't it?"

He looked up and simply nodded his head.

I moved over to sit next to him on the sofa and wrapped my arms around him. Together for the first time in my life, I comforted my father while he cried. I was so thankful that mother was sleeping and shouldn't be awake for a while.

"I can't lose her, Caroline. I can't."

"I know. I understand."

He looked at me through his tears, "And you really do understand this."

"Yes, I do."

"How am I going to tell her?"

"I don't know."

She was so optimistic about this, not saying a negative word about her surgery or treatments. She rarely complained and only commented on how she felt if asked directly.

We sat there holding hands and supporting each other, waiting for mother to be awake. It was not going to be an easy conversation.

"Should I call your brothers to come over?" He asked.

"No, don't bother them yet. This is just a setback. They didn't say she was dying, did he?"

My father looked at me as tears formed in his eyes. He didn't need to say the words. This wasn't treatable.

"I'll call Larry," I said, standing.

I dialed his number and then relayed the message. He said he would call the others, and they would be over soon. We would wait until they were all here to tell her.

Chapter Twenty-Five: December 1974

When we got the news that my mother's cancer was likely terminal, I knew immediately that I would not be going back to work or my life in New York for a while, if ever. So, while my father stayed with mother, my brother Larry and I went to New York. I would move out of my apartment and turn over all my duties at the foundation.

We rented a moving truck and headed out on the road.

"I think this is the first time we've done anything alone," I said.

"Hm, I think you're right." He thought, "That's a shame, but I guess with ten years between us, we haven't been very close, have we?"

"No, but it's time we change that." I smiled.

"Agreed."

"I really appreciate your help."

"Of course, baby sis." He teased.

Hours later, we pulled into the city, and I felt closer to my brother than I had in my life. He was a neat guy, and I enjoyed hearing about his children. I smiled, wondering what Andrew would be like now. He would have been nearly the same age as Denise Ann, Larry's oldest.

She'd just turned six years old, and she liked to talk to me on the phone. We would talk for an hour or more some days. She was smart as a whip. I enjoyed talking to her as much as she liked talking to me.

We parked as close to my apartment building as possible with the box truck and headed in. It had been a while since I'd been here. I walked into a bit of a mess.

I hadn't thought to ask anyone to water my plants which were the least of my problem. As I hadn't expected to be gone so long, I hadn't thoroughly cleaned out my food.

"Yuck, what's that smell?" Larry said, heading straight for a window.

I opened the fridge and gagged, "Hm, looks like ... everything in here has spoiled."

I grabbed a trash bag and started tossing things away. Larry took it down to the dumpster in the alley while I began scrubbing out the stench.

"Ah, that's a lot better already," Larry commented as he came back. "Where's a good place to grab a bite?"

"Bob's diner."

"Sounds good. Let's go."

After we ate, I showed my brother all over my neighborhood. I was so proud of myself and how I'd adapted to life here.

"This is so very different from where we grew up," Larry said as we strolled past a rowdy group. "You walked this alone?"

"Yeah. It's not bad." I held my head a little higher, knowing I'd impressed my oldest brother. "You want to go to a piano bar? They always have amazing jazz."

"I like the way you think."

I giggled and led the way.

The next day, I had to go into the office. I was going to be meeting with my Vice President, Mike O'Reilly, and my secretary, Judith Bronson. Both would be getting a promotion today. I'd already consulted with Gene Butler, and he'd agreed it was the best plan for me to step away and focus on my mother's care. He also thought they would be perfect in their new roles.

Mike would become the Foundation President, and Judith would go from my assistant to VP. Most people might not be ready for such a leap in responsibility, but Judith had been my right hand since nearly the start of this, and she knew the business inside and out.

While I was at the office, Larry would start hauling my furniture to one of the secondhand shops to sell it for me. He had the list of what I wanted to go and what I would be taking home with us. He was also tasked with finding moving boxes.

"Look at my baby sister all dressed up like an executive or something."

"Ha, I am."

"Yeah, that just blows me away. You've done so well for yourself."

"Well, I think you have done pretty well for yourself as well, and at least you're married with children."

"Oh, Caroline, I don't mean ...."

"I know. I'm fine with it." I sighed, "I'm still young. Who knows what my future holds?"

With that, I left to take the two buses to my office for the last time. I laughed when my first bus was late.

"It never fails," I said to one of the other passengers.

"You know it." He replied with a nod.

I arrived at the office and headed to my corner office. People greeted me as I walked. I smiled, but a lump had formed in my throat, and I couldn't speak. This was my dream to help veterans because I couldn't help Walter. It had his name on it. How could I walk away from this?

I knew the answer. It was for my mother. My best friend. She's been there for me over and over. It was my turn to pay her back.

"Knock, knock." Came the male voice at my open office door.

"Oh, hey, Mike, come in," I said and gestured for him to sit.

"Thanks." He sat, "How's it going? How's your mom?"

"She is doing okay at the moment, but the prognosis isn't good." I paused, trying to hold my composer. "And that's why I'm here. I spoke with Gene."

The lump burned my throat, and tears threatened to fall.

"I'm stepping away from the Foundation," I said.

"What? Caroline, you ... you can't. You built this from the ground up. It has *his* name on it."

"I know, but my mother is ... " Tears slowly slipped down my cheek.

"I understand." He passed me a tissue. "So, what does that mean for the Foundation?"

"Well, that's why I asked to speak with you. I would like to offer you the president position."

"Me? Wow. Hm, thank you."

"Do you accept?" I asked, hopefully.

"Of course! I have big shoes to fill, but I will carry on your mission."

"Great. I know you will do wonderful things."

"So, then who will take VP?"

"Well, hold on to your hat because I'm proposing a big one." I took a deep breath, "Judith."

"That is a big one, but yes, I agree. She can handle it."

"Wonderful. Want to tell her with me?"

"Absolutely." He said.

I stuck my head out the door and called her in. She stood, grabbing her notepad, which she usually had with her.

"Oh, you won't need that this time," I said.

"Are you sure?"

"Yes, come on." I giggled a little. She smiled and bounced over to see what my big secret was.

"Oh, hi, Mike." She sat in the other guest chair, "What's going on?"

"So, I just let Mike know, but I am stepping away to take care of my mother."

"Caroline, no, you're the heart and soul of this place."

"No, it is all of you. Not just me." I smiled. This news was happy, and after admitting I had resigned, it got easier to say out loud. "I just offered Mike my position."

"That's wonderful. You'll be great, and I'll be lucky to assist you."

"Actually, you won't be his assistant."

"Am I getting fired?" Tears formed in her eyes.

"Oh, no, nothing like that. We'd like to offer you the vice president position."

"To me? I'm ... I'm a secretary."

"You are so much more than that. You've been my right hand for all these years. I couldn't have done any of this without you."

"I'm speechless."

"But do you accept?" I asked.

"Yes! Of course."

We talked about salary, direction for the foundation, and logistics for their promotions. Unfortunately, I would only be in the city for another day as I needed to get back to my mother.

"I'm reachable if you have questions, but I know you both will do wonderfully and keep things moving forward here."

An hour later, I was holding my personal things in a box and waiting at the bus stop. Finally, the lump in my throat was gone, and relief coursed through my body. That task was done, my goodbyes had been said, and I was on to the next chapter, though it was a potentially sad one, but I was ready.

Chapter Twenty-Six: May 1975

The handbell rang from down the hallway. I checked the time; it was pain medicine time. I put my book to the side and headed to the kitchen to gather them.

The doctors had put her on an experimental drug in hopes she could beat the odds. Part of that was strong pain medicines. But, unfortunately, it was taking a toll on her body. She was a ghost of the woman she had once been. She'd lost so much weight, she almost literally looked like a skeleton with skin stretched over it. She'd lost all of her hair. I barely recognized her these days.

But she was fighting with all her might.

"I have too much to fight for." She told me one day while we were heading to one of her many doctor's appointments.

"You do, mama, and I'll be right here with you."

That felt like years ago, but it had only been last month. Here we were nearing the end; I could feel it.

A nurse came in twice daily to check on her and monitor her vital signs, but the rest of her care was up to my father and me. I took the duties seriously and with a can-do attitude. If she was going to fight, I would fight with her.

I hesitated now outside her bedroom. That positive attitude had faded over the months and weeks, and seeing my once beautiful, healthy mother as a walking corpse was heartbreaking. Just seven short months ago, she was full of life, but now we were just keeping death at bay while we waited on a miracle.

The bell rang again. I sighed and opened the door, plastering a smile as I came into the room. But, internally, I was cringing. She was pale and hollow, looking so much worse than before her nap.

"Did you have a nice nap?"

"No." Her voice was barely audible.

"Here, I've got your medicine." I helped her sit up enough to sip her water and swallow her pills.

She nodded to me once it was down. Then, she slipped back on her pillow, closing her eyes as soon as her head touched it.

I set the glass down and took my seat next to her bed. I held her hand and watched her breathing. Though I was trying to be hopeful, I knew her time with us was getting shorter and shorter. I'd need to let my brothers know. They would all want to be here.

But I didn't move yet. I just watched her and thought. Thought of all the happy moments, all the sad. The smell of fresh-baked cookies when I'd come home from school or when she'd have a tissue handy for the days I'd come home in tears. The whirling sound of her sewing machine and the sound of shears cutting through fabric were sounds of my childhood that I could still hear in my mind, even though she hadn't been able to work in months.

She squeezed my hand, "What are you thinking?"

"Oh, just remembering when you'd sew."

She smiled and nodded, "I miss it."

"You can do it again, as soon as you're better." I tried to be optimistic for her.

"Oh, sweetheart, I won't get better." She whispered.

"Don't say that, mama. You just need to rest."

"I'm tired."

I didn't reply. There wasn't anything to be said. She'd fought a good fight, but I wasn't ready to say goodbye. I wasn't ready to let her go.

I kissed her head gently, "I'll be back soon, mama. Rest now."

I left the room, shutting the door quietly behind me. Without consulting with the nurse, I knew what the next steps needed to be. I wanted to talk to my father and then call my brothers to come over. It was time to let her go.

I found him in the garage. He looked up and simply nodded. I turned back to the house and called Larry. He said he would call the others, and they would be over soon. After hanging up with Larry, I called our pastor and then our nurse. Both said they were on the way.

I then called Frannie. She had asked to know when.

"Hello." Came my friend's comforting voice.

"Hi, Fran, It's Caroline."

"Is it time?"

"It is."

"I'll get with Norm, and we will be on the first available flight."

"Thank you."

With the calls done, I went to sit with my mother for likely one of the last times. I took her hand and sat quietly next to her, listening to her shallow breathing.

I was so thankful to be here these last months. It truly was a blessing, if nothing else. We had that gift of quality time together. But no matter how much time we had, it didn't feel like nearly enough.

"Oh, mama, I'm not ready," I whispered and dropped my head.

She caressed my hand lightly with her thumb. I looked at her to see she was smiling at me.

"I thought you were asleep," I said.

"Oh, I have plenty of time for that." She inhaled and exhaled slowly, "I'm so very proud of you. You have done amazing things, and I know you will continue to."

"Mom ... "

"I wish for you to find love, to find another person you can love even half as much as Walter. Please don't be alone anymore."

"I don't know," I paused, "I'll try."

We sat quietly for a while. She dozed on and off, but we didn't talk again.

The nurse arrived, checked her vitals, and confirmed that it would likely be soon.

"In my experience, I'd say hours at most, but I have a call into the doctor so he can confirm." She made some notes, "I'll stay until the end."

A while later, my father came in with the pastor. He read scripture and said a prayer over her.

"Our thoughts and prayers are with you, Dale. The church is here for anything you all need."

"Thanks, we will be in touch about services."

Once that was done, my father walked him out.

Then he came back, hugged me, and then we both sat next to her, holding hands, and waiting. Then Dean arrived. He whispered to her and then took a seat at the foot of the bed.

Larry and Mary Jane join us. Larry went to her while Mary Jane stood by me, wrapping our arms around each other.

"Where are the children?" I asked.

"My parents." Mary Jane said. I nodded.

Lastly, Karl and Jan came in. Jan joined Mary Jane and me in a hug while Karl said his final words.

We were all together, sitting with her to show our love to her and each other.

Mother looked around at each of us, but her eyes seemed almost hollow. There was no life left in them.

"Connie, I know you are tired. We all love you, but it's okay to rest now." His voice cracked as he spoke.

"We love you, mom," Larry said.

"We'll be okay here. Rest." Karl added.

Dean and I held each other's hands, but neither of us could speak. I tried, but nothing came out. Luckily, I had said everything I'd wanted to say over the past several days, weeks, and months. She knew.

She closed her eyes, and we stood there watching her breath. Suddenly her eyes opened, "Caroline, where's Caroline?"

"I'm here." I went quickly to her side.

"It's Andrew. He's here for me."

I gasped and looked at my father. Tears were streaming quietly down his face.

"Oh, Caroline, he is beautiful." She whispered, "I'm coming, Andrew. Wait for me."

She exhaled slowly and was gone.

Chapter Twenty-Seven: August 1975

I was sitting at the airport bound for London, Paris, and Rome, among my many planned destinations. I had no strict itinerary and no traveling companion to worry about. This was the much-needed break I needed after this last year. My usual safe place to land had changed forever.

It took us several weeks before my father was ready to clean out the house of her belongings. First, we started with the medical equipment and supplies that had piled up. Next, we sorted through her clothing. Most we donated to a woman's shelter.

Then it was time for her sewing room. I stood at the door, staring around the once happy room. I could almost hear the whirl of the machine, the snip, snip of her shears. I touched an unfinished project on the wide table. The delicate pink floral fabric would never be a completed quilt.

"She was so excited about this one." My father said, coming into the room, picking up one of the squares, "She was making it for Denise Ann."

"If I knew how to sew, I'd finish it for her." I laughed, "I can reattach a button, but that's about it."

"She wants me to give it to Leonora to finish." He started to stack the pieces.

"Leonora does lovely work." Not as beautiful as my mother would do, but her friend was a close second. They used to do large pieces together.

We worked quietly for a few hours as we loaded fabric, ribbons, and spools of thread into boxes. They would go to Leonora, who would dole them out to their sewing circle.

Once the house was cleaned, my father settled into his new routine, and I planned my trip. This was something my mother had wanted for me. She had left instructions with my dad to buy me an airline ticket to Europe and fund my trip.

"She needs an adventure after all she has gone through. Helping me, losing both Walter and Andrew. And she works so hard."

Apparently, there was a savings account set up when I was born. It was intended for my wedding, but now 28 years old, and I have no husband and no prospects. So that leads to them transferring it to me upon her death to take this journey.

The plan had been for Frannie to join me, but she recently found out she was pregnant and was having a difficult time with it, so she was advised to stay home. However, she insisted I still go, so I promised to take a lot of pictures and send postcards and that we would go back someday, just the two of us.

Hearing that my best friend was pregnant had stirred emotions inside me. The memories of my one and only pregnancy played on a loop in my mind each night. Remembering the moment that I realized I was pregnant, the first feelings of baby movement, and then the emptiness after he was born.

She had hesitated to tell me, but she couldn't avoid it with having to cancel the trip.

"Oh, Fran, I'm so happy for you and Norm. You will be wonderful parents."

"Are you okay?"

"Of course, I'm thrilled for you both."

"I'm so glad to hear. I had worried the news would upset you."

"I can't hide from children, and you have a right to be happy and start your own family."

"I love you, Caroline."

"I love you too."

I was happy for them. They would be amazing parents. Norm with his quick wit and fun-loving spirit, and Frannie with her nurturing and patience.

However, despite my joy for them, I dreamed of my sweet boy that night. In this dream, he was five years old, and we were at the beach. It felt so real. I could almost feel the sea breeze in my hair, the sun in my face as I squished my feet in the warm sand with little Andrew at my side building a sandcastle.

As he played, he would giggle and look at me with a smile. One dimple just like his father.

As dreams do, this one evolved, and soon the waves grew closer and closer, deeper and deadlier. The beautiful beach day slowly turned into a nightmare, and panic set in as I realized the waves were swallowing him. I reached for him as the waves engulfed him and watched helplessly as he slipped away.

I woke with a scream, my heart pounding and drenched in sweat. I sat there catching my breath and steadying myself. I looked around, knowing it was a dream, but it felt so real that I almost expected to be sitting in the beach chair in my red bikini, watching my son drift away.

I pushed the covers back and made my way to the kitchen for a glass of water.

"Oh, hi, dad." He was sitting at the kitchen table, head in his hand and a glass of water in front of him.

"What're you doing awake?"

"Bad dream. You?"

"Same."

I went to the cabinet, selecting my mother's favorite drinking glasses. I ran my thumb over the delicate frosted pattern. So familiar yet now felt almost foreign without my mother here. I turned on the tap to fill it then joined my father at the table.

We sat there in our mutual grief. No words were necessary as we sat there. Minutes ticked by before either of us spoke.

"Are you looking forward to your trip next week?"

"Yes, I am." I looked at him, "Will you be okay here while I'm gone?"

He looked up, a sadness in his eyes, but he smiled at me, "Of course. I've got my projects and your brothers. Larry and I are going to play golf, Dean said we'd go fishing one day, and Karl is meeting me for dinner one night."

"Oh, good."

I'm glad my brothers were here. Even though I was the youngest, a lot of mother's care had fallen to me. Maybe it was because of the delicate, intimate care she had required, or maybe because I wanted to. But at least my brothers could help my father through his grief. Grief I knew from experience wouldn't go away, but the rawness of it would subside with time.

"Welp, I'm going to bed. Good night." He kissed my head, a gesture he hadn't done in many years. I smiled up at him and then watched him leave the room.

And, now, a week later, I sat in the airport waiting to board a plane for a solo trip to heal myself.

"Thank you, mother," I whispered, trying not to be heard by those around me.

I opened my book back up to try and read, but my body buzzed with excitement and anticipation.

"We will now start boarding flight BA0188 from New York to London at Gate 42."

I stowed my book in my bag and gathered my belongings, then made my way to line up with the other passengers, ready to sip tea and eat biscuits and just relax my mind.

Chapter Twenty-Eight: March 1976

I was again at an airport, but I was making my way from the gate to baggage claim in Houston, Texas, this time. I was here to see Frannie and Norm. Their first baby was due any day now, and I wanted to be here when he or she made their debut into the world.

The airport was bustling but not nearly as busy as in New York. It was a nice change. People here looked at you and smiled or greeted you. I liked that.

Arriving at baggage claim, I checked the board and then oriented myself to where each carousel was.

"That way," I said to myself. Someone standing nearby nodded and grinned at me. "Sorry, long flight."

"No, I get it." He said. "Travel to or from?"

"To here from NYC."

"Ah, well welcome."

"Thanks so much." I smiled, "So I take it you are from here?"

"Yes, ma'am. Born and raised. I had a business trip out in Oklahoma."

His soft Texas drawl was sexy and intoxicating. I wanted to keep speaking to him, so I could hear it. Of course, it helped that he was drop-dead gorgeous with dark, wavy hair and nearly smoke gray eyes.

"Nice."

"Well, Miss... umm?" He cued.

"Caroline. I'm Caroline." I blushed.

"Hi, Caroline. Nice to meet you. I'm Steven."

We stood there a second in awkward silence until I noticed the carousel where my baggage would arrive started to come to life. He followed my eye line.

"You're baggage?"

"Yes."

"I'll let you get to it." He gestured.

I smiled and started to walk away, but before I got more than a few steps, I had a moment of bravery or stupidity. I couldn't believe what I was about to do.

"Um, Steven?" He had already started to walk away.

"Yes?" He faced me with a smile as big as Texas.

"I'll be staying with my friends in Glenn Lake for a while. Maybe we could have dinner sometime while I'm here?"

"Well, isn't this a crazy coincidence? I'm going to Glenn Lake as well." He chuckled.

"That is a crazy coincidence. So, any good restaurants?"

"There is a brand-new Mexican food restaurant. We can meet there one night."

"That would be great. Here let me give you my friend's number." I pulled out a scrap piece of paper and jotted down the Dailey's number, "Now, she's about to have a baby, so things might be chaotic, but I'm sure I'll have free time."

"Are your friends Norm and Frannie?" He said after looking at the number.

"You know them?"

"I do. Norm and I work together, and we're great friends."

"Well, this coincidence just gets crazier, huh?"

"It does." He paused then asked, "Say, do you have a ride down there?"

"I was going to take a cab."

"That will cost too much. I got my truck here, and we're going the same way."

I hesitated for a moment. I didn't know this person from Adam, but it might be safe if he knew the Daileys.

"Sure, let me grab my bag, and then I'm going to just give Frannie a quick call so she knows I'm on my way."

"No problem. Let me help you with your things."

We walked to where the luggage was now being piled up. I pointed to the one that was mine. It had gotten a lot of use lately. My month away had been broken up with a week in London, Paris, and Rome. The final week, I backtracked through until I was once again in London for my last few days.

I felt lighter, more relaxed, and the pain wasn't as raw. But I felt my mother with me every step of the way. When I stood looking out over the River Thames or under the Eiffel Tower, she was there.

"Oh, mother, I miss you every day. Thank you for this trip."

My favorite things were the museums, full of art and history. I had spent countless hours strolling, soaking in the culture. I had delicate teas, delicious wines, and dark ales. I tasted all types of cuisines, from salty to savory. Plates of seafood, various pastas, pastries of all kinds. Thankfully, those bites and sips didn't go straight to my hips due to all the walking I did.

Along the way, I also met so many new people. I actually grabbed a pint with an older couple from Florida, newlyweds from Spain, and a group of single ladies. They were fun, and we exchanged addresses to keep in touch once we all returned to the States. I had provided my father's address, letting them know I haven't settled in any one place yet.

Steven followed me towards the payphones but then was respectful to stand away so I could make my call in private. I looked over at him and smiled as I dialed, then I turned so he couldn't see my face.

"Hello?" Norm said, answering on the second ring.

"Hi, Norm. It's Caroline."

"Caroline! How the heck are ya? Are you at the airport?"

"I am. Just landed. Say, I meet a friend of yours, Steven ... um, something .... "

"Hanson? Just flew in from Tulsa?"

"Yeah, that's him."

"Good guy. He's from Glenn Lake too."

"He offered me a ride, so I just wanted to let you guys know that I was on my way."

I didn't want to admit that despite trusting Mr. Butler all those years ago when I was crying in the diner and then following blindly back to his office and then running all over Europe with strangers just a few months ago, I was cautious here.

"Great! Fran can't wait to see you. She's resting now."

"Well, I'll be there soon."

We hung up, and I turned towards Steven.

"Ready?" I said with a smile.

"Did they tell ya I'm an okay guy?"

I laughed nervously, "Yeah, sorry about that."

"No, I get it. I have a sister. I wouldn't want her taking a ride from some guy she just met randomly."

"Thanks."

I followed him out of the airport through the parking lot to his truck. It was a huge extended cab Chevy. I'd not seen such a large truck before. I looked around to see more trucks than cars.

"Does everyone in Texas drive a truck?" I asked.

"Hm, huh. I never thought about it, but there are a lot of them." He said, loading our bags into the backseat of the truck. He then put his hand out to help me up into the cab.

"Why, thank you," I said as I settled in the front.

He then walked around to the driver's side and hopped in. When he brought the truck to life, it roared, and I could feel it rumbling all around me. It was the perfect Texas welcome.

"Alrighty, let's head to Glenn Lake." He said with a smile.

We drove roughly twenty minutes from the airport south. I watched out the window, taking in every sight. Not that there was a lot around. It was mostly cows.

We chatted easily as he drove. He was a sweet guy, and I'm glad I'd accepted the ride from him. I told him about my life in New York, and he told me about his job.

"Oil and gas is a scary industry, especially right now, but as I'm on the technology side of it, working with computers mostly, so I have a little more job security."

"Computers, huh? That's advanced."

"Yes, but I love a good challenge, and things are evolving nearly every year."

He turned, and I saw a small town come into view. It was beautiful and nearly took my breath away. Please let this be it.

"So here we are, Glenn Lake. It is an up-and-coming little town."

He drove the truck through the main street and around the town square. It was quaint and sweet. People waved as we went by. He named a few of them.

"This is definitely different than New York." Even though I was from a small town originally, it was nothing like this.

"I bet." He turned left, and he pointed to a body of water straight in front of us, "That's Glenn Lake. The town is named for it."

The glistening lake was surrounded by tall pine trees and wide oaks, and many other trees I didn't know the names of. He turned back towards the square and then to an area just behind downtown.

There was the subdivision that the Daileys had mentioned. I could see all the new construction and lots still for sale.

"Wow, they were serious about the size of some of these homes. Way larger than the one-bedroom apartment that I used to live in."

We pulled in front of a brown brick house. It was a ranch-style home. Next to it was a craftsman-styled home with a wide porch, and next to that was an empty lot.

"I live two blocks over." He looked to our right, "You can almost see it from here, but they are building that one there, or you could."

"Nice."

We climbed out of the truck just as the front door opened and out waddled my heavily pregnant friend.

"Oh, you're here. You are finally here!" She called as she made her way down the long sidewalk to the curb. Norm came out behind her.

"Hey, Steven, my man."

"Norm the storm."

The two men greeted each other. Clearly, they were good friends.

"Only you could find one of the few friends Norm has," Frannie whispered to me.

"Yeah, small world for sure."

"Come in, come in." She said, "You too, Steven."

"I can only stay a minute. I haven't been home in a week, and I'm ready to watch television in my favorite chair." He opened the back door of his truck and grabbed my bag out of it.

We walked into their home. My friend had worked hard to make it their own. I could see her in the trinkets and pictures. The yellow and green curtains in the kitchen were the same ones we had in our shared apartment. She had found them at a resale shop and had fallen in love with them.

"This is a beautiful home, Frannie," I said.

"Thank you. We love it. Definitely beats that tiny apartment on West 87th."

"Yes, it does."

"Here, I put you in our guest room." She pushed open the door to reveal a large room with a bed between two windows. It had the quilt my mother had made for them draped over the foot of it.

"Oh, it's one of my mother's creations." I walked to it, touching her tight stitching.

"It is my favorite thing in here."

There was a matching dresser on one wall and a door on the other. Angled in one corner was a mustard yellow armchair. I set my purse on it as Steven stepped in with my large bag.

"Here you are."

"Thank you. I really appreciate you driving me here."

"Not every day I get to come to help a beautiful woman." He winked and then smiled over at Frannie. "Well, I will be in touch."

With that, he left, and I started my first day in Glenn Lake.

Chapter Twenty-Nine: April 1976

I woke to a baby crying, and it took my brain too long before I realized it was Ashley, Frannie, and Norm's newborn daughter. She was born nearly three weeks old and was perfect.

I heard her cries subside. No doubt Frannie was with her.

I had to pee, so I stumbled next door to the bathroom. After I was finished, I went to the kitchen for some water.

"Oh, Caroline, I'm sorry if she woke you."

"Why are you in the living room feeding her?" She usually feds her in their bedroom.

"She was waking Norm, and I wanted him to sleep. Plus, the lighting is better here, and I can see her sweet face."

"She is so perfect," I whispered as I lightly touched her soft head.

"I think so."

"Do you need anything while I'm up?"

"Water? Maybe a few crackers?" She laughed a little, "I'm always so hungry. I thought it would stop once she was born."

"It takes a lot to feed these little ones." Not that I knew from experience. Andrew had been formula feed during his short life.

I went into the kitchen and got us each a glass of water, then I cut up an apple and sliced a few pieces of cheese for Frannie. She needed more than a couple of crackers.

I carried it back in as she switched the baby to the other breast. I set the plate next to her on the side table and the glass next to it. Then I took a seat on the sofa.

"Oh, you're the best. Thank you." With her free hand, she grabbed a slice of apple and added a piece of the cheese to it. "This is way better than a cracker."

"I thought it might be."

"So, what are your thoughts on staying in Glenn Lake?"

I'd been here for nearly a month now, and the conversation had come up a few times, especially since I was dating one of their best friends. Dating was a strong word. We'd gone to dinner twice and lunch once. Plus, he'd showed me around town as well.

I had essentially nothing to go back for. My father had just sold his house and moved in with Larry and his family. Mary Jane had told me he was also seeing a woman but didn't want me to know.

After all, I had done for him, he wanted to keep secrets. Fine. He was an adult, and he could tell me in his own time. The rest of the family knew only because they were there.

All that to say, it didn't feel like home any longer. I didn't have that sense of security and happiness that I once felt. The warm cookie welcome and hug from my mother were gone.

"Steven took me over to the sales office yesterday. I saw a few designs I liked."

"So that sounds promising like you want to stay."

I looked over at the baby, who was now sleeping soundly in her mother's arms. I wanted to watch her grow up. Wanted to watch my friend be a mother, share memories and laughs.

Again, with no job and no strong ties in either Virginia or New York, what did I have to go back to. Here I had a lot of potential happiness and could begin a new life.

"Yes, yes, I'm definitely thinking about staying. I think I'll go back to talk to the salesman tomorrow and finalize the deal. Then I'll work on getting a job here." I had already looked through the want ads in the newspaper.

"Yay! I'm so happy." She cheered quietly. "Well, I'm going to put this little one to bed. Good night, Auntie Caroline."

"Night, little Ashley."

I sat on the sofa for a few minutes, thinking about life. Glenn Lake was such a welcoming place. I had been accepted by the many neighbors as if I'd lived here my whole life.

Steven had been fantastic too. He was thoughtful and sweet, quick-witted, and smart. We'd had a fun day as he helped me look through the available floor plans.

"This one is nice. Not too big with great flow from the front door." I said, looking at a craftsman-styled home. I liked those better than the ranch style. The builders for this neighborhood did both.

Thinking about the houses now, I knew I was making the right decision.

Steven picked me up the next day, and we headed back to the sales office. I still had money from my mother and in my savings account from when I was working. It should be enough to get a house and start my life here.

"I'm so glad you've decided to stay, Caroline," Steven said on the drive over.

"Yeah, I'm excited too. This is a wonderful town, and I love being close to Norm and Fran."

"Do you know which house you're going with?"

"Yes, the 3-bedroom craftsman, and I'm thinking that lot on Harvest Lane."

"Lot 18?"

"That's the one."

"I just met your neighbors. The Walkers. Beth and Wade."

"Oh, nice. I can't wait to meet them myself."

We pulled up at the sales office. A couple hours later, I was a new homeowner, or at least I would be in about six months or so. It was fun picking all the fixtures and elements that would make up my new place. Now I would have to find a temporary place to live until it was ready.

"I'll have to find something to rent until it's ready. I can't stay with Norm and Frannie until then."

"I know there are a few rentals in the downtown area."

"Great. I'll start calling around to see if I could do a short lease."

I wasn't surprised, but oddly disappointed, that Steven hadn't suggested I live with him. I knew I wasn't actually ready for that step, nor was our relationship, but the gesture would have meant a lot.

We headed from the sales office to the grocery store. I was cooking pork chops, potatoes, and cabbage for dinner tonight. To help out my friends, I tried cooking for them most nights.

I loaded the cart with all the items I'd need. I hadn't been to the store except for one other time as Norm had been doing the shopping for us.

"Well, hello, Steven." A store employee said.

"Hey Rich, how's the family?"

"Good, good." He turned towards me, "I don't believe I've had the pleasure."

"Oh, Rich, this is my girlfriend, Caroline. She just signed on a new house here."

"Wonderful. Welcome to Glenn Lake. I'm Rich Donovan. My family owns this store, so you'll see me here all the time."

"It's nice to meet you, Rich, and thank you. I look forward to living here."

He had an employee ring up my groceries, and then we left. Rich waved as we went out the door. Then back out on the street, Steven was greeted by another resident.

"Wally, how's life?"

"Wonderful, Steven."

"I want to introduce you to my girlfriend. This is Caroline. She'll be moving here soon."

"Oh, welcome to our quaint town."

"Thank you, and nice to meet you," I said.

A dark-haired woman walked up and put her arm around him. She looked like she had just stepped off the runway from a fashion show. She was slim and tall.

"Caroline, this is my wife, Eloise." Wally said, and then to her, "This is Caroline. She'll be a new neighbor."

"Wonderful to meet you, Caroline." She had a slight English accent.

"Wonderful to meet you as well." I smiled.

"Well, we must be going. We need to pick up our children, but again welcome." Wally said, and they left hand in hand.

This place had already been so welcoming, and with each person I met, I felt better about my decision to stay. However, I never felt this comfortable back home, or at least not since my mother passed or in New York City.

Later back at the Dailey's, Frannie kept me company while I cooked, and she was feeding Ashley.

"I'm so excited about your new house. That lot is so close to ours." She said.

"It is, and I think the floor plan will work for me."

"So, do you think it will just be you in that house?"

I stopped stirring my cabbage for a moment and looked at her. It was still way too early to consider us more than casually dating or to even picture a future with him.

He had his own place, and we never talked even once about me living with him. Not even now, as I would be looking for a rental.

"Yes, at least at first."

She nodded, and I continued cooking. She settled Ashley in a swing, so she was close by.

"Well, I'm just happy you'll be here." She said, coming to put an arm around me.

"Me too." I hugged her back.

"What are you going to do for work, income?"

"I don't know yet. I still have savings by the grace of God, but it won't last long."

"Yeah, I understand that."

"I've been eyeing things in the want ads and have a few jobs that I'm going to apply for, especially now that it's official that I'm staying."

She gave a little squeal. "As talented as you are, someone will snap you up quickly."

"Oh, I hope so."

Chapter Thirty: October 1976

I loved living above the bakery. It always smelled so wonderful, especially in the early morning when Mae and Mary, a mother-daughter duo, would start baking. I found this place just days after signing the contract on my new house.

They had recently opened the shop, including renting out the apartment above. The daughter, Mary, was still relatively young but ambitious and an excellent baker. So when Mae's husband was killed in a truck driving accident, they opened the bakery to support themselves.

At sixteen years old, Mary was quite a spitfire and a hard worker. She had started baking goodies at Christmas time to sell for extra money. So, when her father died, it was an easy leap to open the bakery. But this is why they had named it after her.

They rented the apartment as it came with the building, and they didn't need it. This worked out perfectly for me.

It reminded me of ones in New York, except it was quieter, and the view was amazing. I could see Glenn Lake from my bed. I stretched and looked at the glistening water. It was beautiful with the sun just starting to shine over the water, birds waking. I could see them flitting around in the trees.

Today was the Fall Festival in town. It was celebrated just before Halloween each year, or so I was told. I'd learned the residents love to have fun. There was some festival or another nearly every month. I had enjoyed each one, and it gave me a chance to get to know many of my new neighbors. The Dixons, the Martins, the Walkers, and so many others.

So far, since I'd arrived in March, there had been one for Easter, Memorial Day, Fourth of July, and Labor Day festivals. Next up, they would have one between Thanksgiving and Christmas. Then a big New Year's Day one.

I dressed in my homemade witch costume, which was mostly a black dress, purple tights, and a witch's hat. I then headed down to the bakery as I'd offered my help with their booth today. I couldn't wait to see all the children dressed.

The bell rang through the store as I went in.

"Hello," Mae called out from the kitchen. "We'll be right there."

"It's just me, Mae."

"Oh, Caroline, come on back," She replied.

Mae was a large woman, not just in height but her overall size. She had a booming voice that commanded a room, yet her vibe was nurturing and comforting. She felt like everyone's mother.

"Caroline Graham reporting for duty," I said when I entered the kitchen.

They both laughed.

"We are just packing everything into these white boxes, and then the bakery boxes go into these crates," Mary said as she handed me an apron and plastic gloves.

We worked for an hour getting all the baked goods put safely away to be transported down the street to where the booth would be set up. We then got those loaded onto a large, flat wagon that they had. Next, we packed a box with decorations in it. Lastly, Mae grabbed a cash box. Each child would get one free cookie of their choice, and everything else was for sale.

"Alright. I think that's everything."

We walked along the sidewalk and into the town square. People were hustling and bustling about getting the town square all set up for the ghosts, witches, and ghouls that would be arriving in a few hours.

"Hey, Rich." Mae greeted the grocer as we arrived. He was holding a clipboard and dressed up as a vampire.

"Oh, hey, Mae, Mary, Caroline." He looked down at the clipboard, running his finger down the list until he found what he was looking for, "Mary's bakery, you are in booth 10 next to ... Ron's diner." He looked up and smiled.

"Thanks!" Mary giggled. "I'm so excited."

We headed to our booth, greeting neighbors along the way. We arrived to find two 6-foot tables with a pop-up tent covering us from the Texas sun because even though it was October, it was still shining brightly and somewhat hot.

We spread out the tablecloths with their fun pumpkin print, and then they had some plastic pumpkins, a witch figurine, and a black cat. Mary laughed and giggled the whole time.

"I can't believe this is our first Fall Festival. Of all the events we've done so far, I've been looking forward to this one the most." She said as she began unloading the cookies.

"Me too," Mae added.

"I never asked. When did you open?"

"In February. Our first one was the Valentine's Day fair, and we've done them all since." Mary grinned with pride.

"How lovely. So, I haven't missed much."

"Well, no, just Valentine's, right? You came right after that."

"Yes, that's right. I wish I would have listened to Norm and Fran sooner." I laughed, "I have never felt so at home anywhere."

"Glenn Lake is happy to have you," Mae said, leaning over to hug me.

Soon the crowds started to arrive with the various little trick or treaters dressed in all kinds of fun costumes. There were ghosts, cowboys and cowgirls, and a lot of superheroes. We passed out dozens and dozens of cookies.

Frannie and Norm came with little Ashley in a stroller and dressed as a black cat.

"Oh, look at the little kitten." I cooed to Ashley and picked her up out of the stroller. She loved her Auntie Caroline. "You're the cutest little kitten ever."

"Is your shift here over?"

I looked over at Mae, who nodded that I could go.

"I can come back later if you need help." I offered.

"We never turn down offers to help." Mary teased.

"Well, alright, I'll be back. Let's go have some fun little Ashley."

We walked around the festival, checking out the vendors and visiting with the different residents.

"Oh, it's Wally and Eloise Dixon," Frannie said, waving towards them.

"Look at little Craig. He is a little superman." I said. "Hi, Wally, Eloise."

"Hi, Caroline, Frannie." Eloise said, "And look at how cute Ashley is today."

"Thanks, Eloise. Craig is a cute superman."

"I can fly!" He announced.

"Oh, really?" I said.

"Yes, watch!" He went running and then jumped, arms stretched out.

All the adults cheered for him, as did Ashley. She clapped and squealed, watching him as he proudly did it again and again. Then, after a few more jumps, the Dixons said goodbye and took Craig to the pony rides.

Then as we were walking around, we bumped into the Walkers.

"Oh, hi, soon-to-be next-door neighbor," Beth said. They had bought the house right next to mine. They were about a month ahead in the building process.

"Hi, Beth. Wade. How are you doing today?"

"Doing well." Wade said, "How about you? Enjoying the festival?"

"Yes, it's wonderful. All the children look so cute."

"They are," Beth said, smiling at a few that went by us.

We talked for a few minutes about this booth or that attraction before we parted ways.

"So, where is Steven today?" Frannie asked.

"He is on another trip," I said.

"I'm so glad that Norman doesn't have to travel like that." She said, looking at him with a smile.

"Yeah, I'm lucky for sure. He has to travel a lot." Norm said.

"I hate that he is missing all the fun." I looked around at all the smiling, happy faces.

We walked to Abuelita Carmen's booth and ordered some tacos. Then found a picnic table to eat at.

"Are you glad you moved here?"

"I am. Thanks for always pushing me out of my comfort zone."

"That's what friends are for."

After we ate, they left so Ashley could have her afternoon nap, so I went back to help Mae and Mary. They sold out of everything before the end of the day, which made clean-up so much easier for us. We had a leisurely walk back to the shop.

"There were so many cute kiddos today," I said. "I'm so glad you asked me to join you."

"We were so happy to have your help today, Caroline," Mae said.

"Yes, we appreciated it," Mary added

"Oh, I was happy to do it." I smiled.

We said goodbye, and I went home, ending the first of many Fall festivals in Glenn Lake.

Chapter Thirty-One: February 1977

"And there you go, Caroline," The builder, Matt, said in his long Texas drawl, then handed me the key to my house, "You're a homeowner here in Glenn Lake now."

"Thank you." I clasped those keys proudly.

I had not owned a home yet, having always rented. This was huge. I nearly skipped out of his office.

I clung to the keys as I drove straight over to my house. I sat in the driveway for a moment staring at it.

"All mine."

I hopped out of the car and up the couple of steps to my wide porch. I giggled as I unlocked the front door. Then, swinging the door wide, I took a deep breath.

I inhaled the fresh wood and paint smell. It wasn't unpleasant.

"Ah, that new home smell." Not that I had ever really smelled it before, but that's the best way to describe it.

I went room to room, taking it all in. This was all mine. I'd waited months to see the finished product, though I'd watched them every step of the way.

Steven, Norm, Wally, and Wade were all going to help me move my things from the apartment. Then once I was settled in a few weeks, we were having a housewarming party. I couldn't wait.

"Okay, house, I'll be back in a bit with all your accessories." I laughed as I went out the door.

Back in my apartment, I loaded the last of my belongings into boxes and took the lighter stuff to my car. My friends should all be here soon.

I bounced as I walked to my car and back. I waved to Mae and Mary as I passed the bakery window. Terry Eastman was sweeping in front of his shop and called out.

"Moving day, Caroline?"

"Yes, it is!"

"Well, it's been nice having you in town. I'll see you around."

I waved and skipped back upstairs, continuing to bring down what could fit in my car. Finally, I put the last box in the car and turned to see Frannie, Norm, and Steven walking towards me.

"Hey!" I waved, "Where's Ashley?"

"Oh, I asked Eloise to watch her so I could help my best friend get moved." She grinned, "It's a big milestone, and I couldn't miss out."

"Aw, you're the sweetest." I hugged her.

"Wade and Wally should be here any second with the truck?" Steven said as he greeted me with a kiss.

"Great."

We waited only a minute before the rental truck rolled up.

"Your chariot has arrived." Wade said with a laugh as he hopped out of the truck, "Well, you know what I mean."

I laughed, "Thanks for bringing it. Are y'all ready?"

We all marched upstairs, and I started directing everyone. We got the truck loaded rather quickly, with only a few disagreements on how and where to put things.

"I'm going to just run back upstairs and make sure everything is off," I said. Frannie stayed behind with me. "We'll meet you over there."

We went back upstairs. Stepping into the empty space, I looked around. I hadn't been here long, but the room had been a wonderful start to my new life.

"This was a nice place." She said as if reading my mind.

"It really was." I smiled, "Reminds me a bit of that place we shared."

"Yes, but I think this is bigger."

"Ha, yes, it is, and cleaner."

"Better neighbors." She added.

We hooked arms and just stood there a moment. She seemed to know when I needed that type of comfort. After a few minutes, I sighed.

"I guess we should get over to the new house."

I double-checked that everything in the apartment was secured, then I ran down to the bakery to leave the keys with Mae. It was her apartment, after all.

"Here, I made these for you." Mary handed me a bakery box full of cookies, "A small housewarming gift."

"Aw, you are the sweetest." I hugged her. "I will miss waking up to this smell every day."

"We'll miss your smiling face in the morning," Mae added.

With that, we headed to my car and to my new home.

I had been in the house for about a month now. It was the perfect fit for me. Not too large, not too small, with three bedrooms, two bathrooms, and a bright kitchen that overlooked the backyard. In the front of the house was a formal sitting area and a formal dining area.

I didn't have the dining area set up yet and couldn't imagine I'd use it much. However, I liked the kitchen and breakfast area's more relaxed and cozy feeling. Baked cookies and hot tea were served from there. What could be more comforting?

I bought a cherry wood table with 6 matched chairs. It fit perfectly in that space, and I could already picture hosting friends for meals, playing cards, or chatting about life with them. I took a pause and looked at it now.

I had covered it with a bright floral tablecloth; even though it was not quite Spring yet, it just felt right for today as I prepared to celebrate with my friends.

The formal sitting area had two armchairs with a round side table between them. Once I placed my mother's milk glass lamp on it, the space became my favorite place to read with a cup of tea and a view of the front yard.

I couldn't wait to update the landscaping in a few months. I imagined roses and beautiful boxwoods. I hadn't had a yard before, so I was looking forward to it. The builder had planted a beautiful magnolia tree in the back for me. I loved it.

Now that everything was unpacked and felt like home, I was having a housewarming party tonight. It was a potluck, so everyone was bringing something. I had made several dips that would be perfect if eaten with crusty slices of bread or veggies dipped in.

There was a knock on the door. It must be Steven. He'd promised to come over early to help grill some chicken and hamburgers. I was so thankful for the excellent weather here that made grilling easy nearly year-round.

I floated to the front door.

"Hi," I smiled as I opened the door, "Do you need help carrying anything?"

"Nope, I got it." He was carrying a large ice chest. "I have my grill in the truck. I'll just take it around through the gate."

I opened the back door for him, and he set the cooler on my back porch. Then, turning towards me, he pulled me in for a kiss. I giggled in his arms.

"I'm so glad I'm not traveling this week. I've missed you."

"I missed you too."

He kissed me again and then headed to get the grill. Once he had it in place, he fired it up to get nice, hot, and ready for cooking.

"Brought you this," I said, handing him a beer.

"Thanks." He smiled, "The place looks really nice. I haven't seen it since you got the kitchen table in, and the front room is good."

"Aw, thanks. Yeah, I love how both of those spaces worked out."

"You have an eye for decorating."

"It's been my favorite place to decorate so far, but I still have a bit to do." I smiled, "I have no idea what I'll do with the extra bedrooms."

"Yeah, I have the same problem."

We both had houses that we couldn't use all the rooms in with no plan or talks of moving in together. We were still barely serious. But, he made a nice companion.

For me, it was the perfect situation as it was all I could handle at current. If we dated like this for years, I would be completely happy.

As far as my house, Denise Ann wanted to visit me for an extended vacation, so at least one room would be a guest room. Perhaps the other would be a hobby room and storage or another guest room. Who knows?

People started to arrive, so I greeted them at the door, and soon my house was party central. The men were in the backyard drinking beer and talking around the grill. A few were throwing horseshoes.

The ladies were split between the back patio and the kitchen. We were uncovering casseroles, salads, and baked goods. I uncorked a bottle of wine.

"Wine anyone?" I offered as I started to fill a few of the wine glasses.

"I'll take one of those." Eloise Dixon said.

"Fran?" I asked.

She looked down at her feet and then up at me with a weak smile, "I can't. I'm pregnant." She giggled.

"Oh, Frannie! Are you serious? That's wonderful." I hugged her, "Why didn't you tell me yet?"

"I only just found out, and I didn't want to steal your day."

Others nearby offered congratulations as well.

"Well, if we are sharing news, I'm pregnant too." My new neighbor, Beth, shared.

"Oh, wow!"

"Congratulations."

"We'll have kids in the same class," Frannie said.

"Thanks. I don't want to jinx us. We have lost one already." She frowned. The pain in her eyes was unmistakable. "But I have a good feeling about this one." She touched her stomach.

I reached my hand out and squeezed her shoulder. I had never told her that I had lost a baby too, but I might share that with her one day. But today was not that day.

The rest of the party wasn't as eventful, just a good evening with friends sharing good food and good news.

Chapter Thirty-Two: April 1977

I'd lived in Glenn Lake for a year, but only a few months in my new house. With Frannie and some new friends, I was able to finish furnishing my home before hosting the housewarming.

I had almost nothing left from my life before this, having sold my furniture and only had a few boxes with pictures, clothing, and unique trinkets left from my life before. Then there were a few large boxes with things I'd saved of my mother's; one was full of quilts. I had them displayed around the house. Then I had her jewelry, photos, and a few special things she had loved.

My father was now living with a woman, and she did not want my mother's things around. I didn't like her at all. I didn't even acknowledge her, and the feeling was mutual. She'd driven a wedge in our family.

I still kept in touch with my sisters-in-law, and if not for them, I wouldn't know anything about my family any longer. My mother had been the glue that held our family together, or so it seemed.

Glenn Lake had become home and my family. Everyone had welcomed me with open arms. There was a sense of community that I hadn't had before. Everyone knew each other, pulled together when needed, and celebrated every win.

My immediate neighbors were Wade and Beth Walker on one side and Joe and Laura Rafferty on the other. Neither family had children yet, so our little section was quiet. However, going over to the street near the Daileys or even on Steven's block, there were children everywhere. I loved watching them.

Little Ashley was toddling around and wanted to play with the other children so badly. There was a girl slightly older who lived next door named Heather. The two girls played together. It was fun to watch my goddaughter growing up and making friends.

I work now at the Houston Chronicle as an editor. It was a job I enjoyed and thrived at, though I had to commute into Houston. It wasn't too bad.

As I was thinking about my life here, there was a knock on my door as I was baking up a batch of cookies for the church bake sale tomorrow. I dusted off my hands and headed for the door.

"Oh, hi, Steven." I said when I opened the door, "I wasn't expecting you until later."

"I know. I'm sorry for not calling first."

"Come in."

"Thanks." He stepped in, and we walked to my kitchen.

"Would you like something to drink?"

"No, thanks." He wouldn't make eye contact with me.

"What's wrong?" I said, taking his hand.

"I was offered a new job."

"Oh, that's fabulous, so what's the problem?"

"It's in California." He pulled away from me a bit.

"Oh."

"Yeah, and I know you just moved here, but ... would you consider moving with me?"

I gasped, "That's huge. I would have to think about it."

"Yeah, that's what I thought." His voice cracked a bit.

"That doesn't mean no. It's just a huge decision. I had just settled into the house a few months ago. I have a job here, and are we that serious? We aren't engaged, married. We aren't even living together." I paused to think about where I was going with this train of thought, "It never even came up in a conversation when I was moving here. I rented over Mary's Bakery for six months while my house was being built."

"That's all true." He went down on one knee, and a ring came out of his pocket, "I thought I would fix that. I love you, Caroline. I think I have since that first day at the airport." I took a deep breath, "Will you marry me?"

"Steven, oh, wow." I stammered. "I ... I don't know."

This was all a lot at once, and I know I pointed out that we weren't married or engaged, but I didn't mean let's do it now. I never even thought of him as much more than a fun companion. I loved him, but did I want to marry him and move away at this point?

His mouth fell open, but he didn't make a move to stand. I could almost hear his heart beating, or maybe that was mine. It was pounding nearly out of my chest.

"You don't know?"

"I'm not great with change or with surprises. I need time to process and think." I wanted to say overthink this, but I didn't. But that's what I meant. I would obsess and overthink until I couldn't decide.

He stood then, putting the ring back, "Okay. Are we still on for dinner later?"

"Yes, I'm looking forward to it."

"Great." He leaned forward to kiss me quickly, "I'll be back then."

He grabbed a cookie from the cooling rack, smiled at me, and then left.

I immediately dialed Frannie. I needed a sounding board.

"Hello?"

"Frannie, I need you."

"I'll be right there."

That was all I needed to say and all she needed to hear to be there for me. I paced around, mumbling to myself. I was a confident woman until it came to love. I wanted to love and be loved, but on the flip side, I didn't want to get hurt. That was my only hesitation. I couldn't go through that grief again. Of loving someone so much, and then they were just gone.

"Knock, knock." Came Frannie's voice at the door.

"I'm back here," I called from the kitchen. I had started some water in the kettle and had two mugs ready for hot tea.

She had little Ashley with her. She squealed when she saw me and toddled over for me to pick her up.

"Hi, sweet girl." I said."

"Auntie K. Auntie K." She couldn't quite say my name yet, but she loved me.

"So, what's wrong?" Frannie asked, taking the hot water off the stovetop and filling each cup. Then grabbed a cookie for Ashley.

"Steven proposed."

"He did what?" She blurted.

"Yes, he came by, said he was moving, and then asked me to not only go with him but if I would marry him."

"And what did you say?" She asked, looking at my hand, "I don't see a ring, so what does that mean?"

"I told him I had to think about it." I put Ashley down, "It is a huge decision. I only just moved here, and then I didn't think we were at that point. Did you?"

She'd known us through our entire relationship. He was friends with Norm, her husband, and we double-dated a lot. We'd play cards together or have cookouts together.

"Well, I don't know... I *am* surprised. That's for sure."

"Me too."

"Can you see yourself married to him?"

"No, and I don't want to move. I really love Glenn Lake." I looked down at Ashley, playing with a few toys that Frannie had stashed here. "And she's my favorite little person."

"So, are you going to turn him down?"

"What do you think I should do?"

She shrugged. We sat with our tea and silently watched the baby babble and play. She had gotten so big over the past year. I had thought watching her grow would remind me of what I'd lost, and while yes, I had some of those feelings, I thoroughly enjoyed these little moments.

She looked up at me and smiled. Her little cherub face lit up. Then, she stood and brought me the stuffed puppy she was playing with.

"Doggy."

"Yes, a little brown and white doggy."

"Woof, woof."

"That's right. A dog says woof, woof."

She giggled and then turned back to her toys.

"That's it." I wiped my hands together, "I know I can't leave her and you and all of this." I finally said.

"When will you break it to Steven?"

"Tonight. We are going to dinner at Abuelita Carmen's."

"Are you still going, or will you tell him before dinner?"

"I should probably do the decent thing and tell him before dinner, right?"

"Yeah, you know it is."

I nodded but didn't say anything.

"How do you keep having these guys proposing to you, and you aren't into them? Are you that good in bed?" Frannie laughed.

"Fran!" I laughed and swatted her hand lightly, "But, seriously, I don't know. After this I doubt, I will date again. This is the last time."

I wasn't putting myself through that. I hated to hurt people, but especially myself.

We visited a bit longer before she had to get Ashley home for her nap. I kissed her little head as Frannie carried her out the door. She yawned and reached for me.

"Bye, sweet girl," I whispered.

I puttered around my house after that. I was putting the finishing touches on my guest room so that my oldest niece could come to visit this summer. Her mother would fly with her here, and then Denise would stay for a month, and then my brother would come to pick her up.

I had big plans for the two of us. We'd spend time at Galveston beach and then picnic at Glenn Lake. After that, we'd do some shopping. I'd also take her to a baseball game or two.

She was a huge baseball fan, which she got from Larry. He played back in high school and into college. She could name players and their stats.

I checked the time and realized it was nearly time for my date. Cue the butterflies in my stomach, but not the happy, excited ones. This was all nerves. I went to my room to freshen up.

"You can do this," I said to my reflection. "It is the right thing."

There was a knock at the door. I turned towards the sound for only a second and then looked at my reflection once more. I took a deep breath and then smiled at myself.

"Hi," I said, opening the door.

"Hey there," He stepped forward to kiss me. Oh gosh, this was going to be difficult. I loved kissing this man, but I did not want to move. I loved it here. "Can we talk?"

"Oh, yes, I wanted to talk to you as well," I said.

I led the way to my kitchen and gestured for him to sit. He sat in his usual spot on the left side of the table, and I took my spot to his right.

We sat there, not speaking for a moment. The tension between us hung heavy in the air. I could almost feel it prickling my skin as goosebumps rose on my skin.

"So, I thought about what you said." He started, "You're probably right."

"I'm right?"

"Yes, we didn't move in together. I thought it was because we had just met, and it was that way, but my instinct wasn't to even ask."

"Yes, we had. It was probably the right thing, but watching Fran and Norm, they wanted to live together almost from day one."

"They are a cute couple." He said.

"I'm sorry."

"Me too." He smiled and took my hand, "You still want to get some dinner? My treat."

"Are you sure?"

"Absolutely. We both still have to eat, right?" He winked.

"Alright, let's go."

This had to be the best and weirdest break-up ever. I got dinner, and we still had a great conversation. Despite that, I intended to stick to my new life and never date again. I was happy with my quiet life.

Chapter Thirty-Three: July 1977

I was waiting by baggage claim for my niece and sister-in-law. Mary Jane would stay a few days, and Denise Ann would stay for a month. I couldn't wait.

I checked the arrival times on the board. They should have landed and would be here any second.

I glanced around, remembering the last time I was here. It's when I'd met Steven. I had heard that he had made it to California. He had no trouble selling his house here, having it sold within a week of putting it on the market.

I was happy for him, but I missed his company and our conversations. However, I know I made the right decision.

"Auntie Caroline!" I heard a sweet voice call to me.

"Denise Annie!" I spun just in time to catch her in my arms as she hurled herself at me. "I'm so glad you're here."

"Me too. The plane ride was fun, but it took us *forever*."

"Hi, Mary Jane, good to see you." I hugged my sister-in-law.

"Good to see you too."

"Let's get your bags and head home."

We headed to the baggage carousel with Denise skipping along beside me. She bounced around as we looked for their bags.

"That's Denise Ann's." She said, pointing at a pink one. It was closer to me, so I grabbed it. "Oh, and here's mine." She grabbed it.

"Any others?"

"One more for Denise."

"There it is, mommy," Denise said, pointing and trying to jump at it. While Mary Jane grabbed the bag, I held her hand tightly. I didn't want her getting caught on the carousel. No accidents on day one.

"Alright, that's it." Mary Jane said.

"Well, then follow me, ladies."

I lead them to my car. On the drive home, I pointed out different sights and told her all my plans for the summer.

"I have tickets to the Astros against the Cincinnati Reds."

"Really? I love baseball."

"I know you do." I winked in the rear-view mirror at her. "I got us good seats too. I can't wait for you to see them."

She wiggled and bounced in the backseat. I was so happy to see her smiling face.

"Wow, it is bigger than I thought." Mary Jane said as we drove from the airport towards Glenn Lake.

"Yes, everything is so spread out, so it makes it feel big."

"I can't wait to see Glenn Lake. The town that got you to move clear across the country."

"It is beautiful. The people are so friendly, and Norm and Frannie are here."

"Ms. Frannie is so nice. I can't wait to see her." Denise Ann said from the back seat.

"She is excited to see you too, and I can't wait for you to meet little Ashley. She is so adorable."

I turned off the freeway, and after several miles, I could see the edge of Glenn Lake. There was the newly built city hall with the clock. I couldn't wait to show them both around.

"Is this it?" Mary Jane said as the town square came into view.

"This is it," I said with pride. I hadn't lived here long, but it felt so much like my home now. A place I felt I belonged.

"It's so beautiful and quaint."

After driving through the square, I took a right off Main Street and down Second Street towards my neighborhood. As we drove, Denise was in the backseat reading all the store signs and street signs. I could feel her excitement radiating from the backseat.

A few more streets, and I was pulling into my driveway.

"Oh, Caroline, you have a beautiful home." Mary Jane said.

We grabbed their bags and then headed inside.

"Well, here we are." I led the way to the bedrooms. "And this will be yours while you're here."

"Oh, Auntie Caroline, this is so pretty." She bounced onto one of the two twin beds.

The beds were made with bright yellow comforters with blue pinstripes running vertically. The wallpaper had a cream-colored background with yellow and blue stripes. Then I had added shiny blue lamps with sunny yellow shapes, and floral artwork hung on the walls. It was inviting and reminded me of Springtime.

"I have you in the next room, and the bathroom is between them." I gestured towards the hallway. She followed me out, and I showed her the two rooms. "I'll let you both get settled, and then we'll head over to meet the Daileys at Abuelita Carmen's."

"Sounds good."

Several hours later, we were being seated at the restaurant. Denise Ann was playing with Ashley.

"Frannie, you are simply glowing." Mary Jane said.

"Thank you. I can't believe I'm having a second little one." She touched her barely showing belly, "Oh, but Caroline, you heard about Beth, right?" She whispered.

"No, what?"

"She lost the baby. The second one, I believe."

"Oh, no. I know she was so hopeful."

The conversation changed directions after that as we talked about other neighborhood gossip and my plans over the next few weeks.

I had been fortunate enough to get the time off from work. I would need to run a few stories up to the office, but for the most part, I didn't have to work.

After dinner, we went for a walk over to the lake. We let Ashley and Denise run around. It was so cute to watch Denise play with the toddler. As I watched my niece, I couldn't help but wonder what Andrew would be like at this age. Would he be patient with the baby, or would he be a rough and tumble boy?

Honestly, I had hoped he would have been a mix of both. A patient, caring boy who could be playful and tough. I smiled at the thought and then looked over again to where my niece was playing. Ashley was giggling and trying to chase after her.

"Are you thinking of Andrew?" Frannie asked as she slipped her arms around me.

"Yes, how did you know?"

"You always look at Denise Ann as if you're watching him too."

"Maybe I am trying."

We stood there for a moment while the children played before we decided it was time to call it an evening. Denise and Mary Jane were still on eastern time, so Denise was yawning as soon as we started to drive towards home.

"I like it here, Auntie Caroline." She said through one of the yawns. "Maybe I'll come to live here one day when I'm big."

"I would love that."

"Oh, no, you don't. You are never leaving me." Mary Jane teased.

"Mommy, you still have Aaron and daddy. Auntie Caroline needs me here."

My heart squeezed. Did she know how much I thought of Andrew when she was around and that I loved her even more for that slight connection? It was a big burden for a little girl, but I had no expectations of her. I simply wanted to enjoy her and imagine.

Honestly, I loved all my nieces and nephews. She was just the first and the closest to Andrew's age, which just gave her a few extra points.

"Oh, sweetie, I love you being here, and if that is what you decide to do with your life, I would happily have you here. But I know your mommy, daddy and Aaron need you there."

"For now, but someday, I'm going to get a job and move here." She crossed her arms over her chest as if to put a sharp period on that statement.

"Well, okay then. I'll always have a room for you here."

Chapter Thirty-Four: August 1977

We were at the end of our summer visit, which meant Larry was coming to collect his daughter from me. As his wife had, he would stay a few days before they flew back, and then Denise Ann would be off to 4th grade.

She was so bright. We had played Scrabble a few times, and she knew so many words, beating me at least twice.

"Are you ready to see your daddy?" I asked as we walked into the airport.

"Maybe."

"Maybe? What kind of answer is that?" I chuckled.

"I just don't want this time with you to end." She held my hand a bit tighter as if it was a lifeline.

"I don't either, but you will love being home in your own bed and getting ready for 4th grade."

"I guess."

I'm so glad she had a good time with me. I haven't had to entertain a child for so long before. It had been exhilarating and exhausting all at the same time.

We waited in my usual spot around the baggage claim area. It was near the stairway that brought people from the terminal. The board showed his flight was on-time and should be landing any second.

We did some people-watching together as we sat on a nearby bench. She had a good imagination and would make up stories about each person.

"Oh, these two are interesting," I said to her. "What do you think their story is?"

The couple looked exhausted with dark circles. Her hair looked a bit frizzy, and she had a few flyaway pieces. His suit looked wrinkled. They were not looking at each other, but you could tell they were together. There was a clear tension between them.

"Hm, well, I think they had an awful vacation. They had flight delays; the airline lost their luggage. The hotel was a dump. Then each blamed the other. Finally, they got in a huge fight and are just happy to be home now." She giggled.

"Wow, that is some story. How did you come up with it so fast?"

"Mommy and daddy sometimes fight when things go wrong like that. We had driven to Virginia Beach, and we got a flat tire on the way. They fought about it the whole trip because the spare tire wasn't in the car. Daddy had left it at home by mistake. Then another time, we were at a hotel, and the toilet overflowed. Mommy said it was an old hotel and the other rooms were having the same problem. We had to switch hotels. They were both upset."

"Are you telling all our secrets, peanut?" Larry's familiar voice sounded from behind us.

"Daddy!" She jumped up and straight into his arms. "I missed you."

I guess she was more excited to see him than she thought. I would truly miss her.

"Hey, Larry," I said, standing to hug him as well.

"Hey, baby sis."

"Do you have any bags?" I looked at the duffel bag he was carrying.

"Nope, actually, this is it."

"Well, let's head home."

Once back in my car, Denise Ann filled her father in on our time together.

"And we went to the beach. Did you know it's not the Atlantic Ocean here? It's the Gulf of Mexico."

"I didn't know that." He said, winking at me. We both knew he did, but why spoil it for her.

"Oh, yes, it's different. We got to have a whole day playing and swimming. Then the next day was the baseball game. That was in the Astrodome, which is amazing. It's all enclosed, and we had seats right behind the dugout. The Astros played against the Reds, and they won."

"The Reds?" He asked.

"No, daddy, the Astros. Everyone cheered. I got to eat a hot dog and popcorn. I also got a t-shirt."

"Nice. What else?"

"We went to this other place called Astroworld. It's across the street from the Astrodome. It's a large amusement park. We got to ride so many rides. They had this roller coaster called the Texas Cyclone, and it was so big. I wasn't scared, though."

"Not even a little?" He teased.

"Okay, maybe a little. It was super-fast." She giggled, "but I loved it. There were games too. I won a stuffed teddy bear."

"It sounds like you had a lot of fun here."

"I did. We played board games almost every night, and we had dinner with Mr. and Mrs. Dailey a lot. I love their baby, Ashley. She is so cute. They are going to have another baby in a few months."

"That's exciting for them."

"And when I'm grown, I'm going to move here too."

"That's what mom said. I hope you do. I always want you to live your dreams."

My heart fluttered at my brother's words. He was a good father.

We had never been close growing up. Even as adults, we rarely talked. If it wasn't for Mary Jane, I wouldn't know anything going on with them.

Though he had helped me so many times over the years, we always had good conversations and fun when we were together. Unfortunately, it was few and far between, so I was really looking forward to these few days with him.

As we pulled into the town square, Denise started pointing everything out to him.

"And that's Mary's Bakery. It is a mother and daughter that run it. Auntie Caroline used to live in the apartment above them. They have the best cookies." She bounced to the other side of the car, "And, down that way is the lake. It has a fun park. We had two picnics there."

"This is a nice-looking town, sis."

"Yeah, I like it a lot. Reminds me a bit of home, but in a different way."

"Dad says hi, and he'd love for you to call him more."

"The phone works both ways."

After all, I'd done for him and mother, I was a little bitter that he would run off with the first woman to bat her eyes at him. He let her control his whole life to the point he couldn't even have a picture of mother anywhere. At least he had sent those to me rather than destroy them.

Larry didn't say anything, but I knew from talking to Mary Jane that he felt the same way, but maybe slightly different.

It wasn't him that had sat up with our mother all those months as she vomited from her treatments or watched her wither away. He also wasn't the one sitting with her as she cried, knowing she was nearing the end. That had been father and me.

The bond I thought my father and I had after losing our special person in life had been broken when he introduced us to Blanche during a Thanksgiving dinner. She was cold to all of us, his children and grandchildren.

She asked if they could leave halfway through dinner as she wasn't comfortable being with us. He apologized but went with her. We had all sat there, confused and hurt. It wasn't long after that that I decided that was not my home any longer.

We pulled into my house and piled out. Larry stood for a moment, looking around.

"This is a nice neighborhood indeed. You've done really nice for yourself here."

I felt pride fill me as I looked around. His words meant more to me than almost anyone else's.

"Thanks. That truly means the world to me."

Chapter Thirty-Five: May 1978

I was at home working on an article for work. I sometimes did this to save me time in the office, and I didn't have to commute. I was thankful that my boss didn't care how I got work done, just that my articles made it in time for printing and that they were error-free.

As I was proofreading the article, my phone rang.

"Hello?"

"Caroline, it's Gene."

"Gene, what a surprise. How are you?"

"I'm well. And you?"

"Can't complain. I have a feeling this isn't a social call."

"It is sort of. Marie and I would like to come to visit you. We have a proposition for you."

"Oh, yeah?"

"I'm going to retire from Groove, and I'd like for you to take it over."

"But that's in New York, and I'm ... not."

"That's okay. If you are in charge, you can move it anywhere you want. Or even run it in both locations. It will be yours to do with what you'd like."

"Wow, I don't know what to say."

"I hope you will accept the offer."

"Oh, yes, I will, but you aren't just giving it. You'll sell it to me, right?"

"Richard has no interest in it, and I have no other children who can take over from me. You may have not been here long, but you know the business, and you ran the Foundation beautifully. So that's my long-winded way of saying, Caroline Graham, Groove Magazine is yours free and clear, if you would like it."

"Okay then, I happily accept."

"Great. Marie and I will fly down in about two weeks. I'll have my lawyer type up all the details. After that, we can discuss it more and then sign it over."

"I'm so excited."

We hung up with him promising to let me know their travel plans.

"I can't believe it! I can't believe it!" I squealed, dancing around the room.

I loved working at Groove for the short time I had. It was my introduction into the workforce, and I tried to soak up every bit of knowledge I could. Though at first, I was stuck in the typist pool fixing copy. Later working for Sally and Bert had been where I learned the most.

I had been allowed to sit in on brainstorming meetings, and Bert took a lot of time to teach me what they do. The experience had allowed me to easily step into my current job at the Houston Chronicle. In fact, it helped me with running the Foundation.

I picked up the phone.

"Hello?"

"Hey, Frannie, guess what?"

"What's going on?"

"Gene Butler called me and has offered Groove Magazine to me. He and Marie are coming here in two weeks to finalize it."

"Oh wow! That's huge." There was a slight sound of a baby fussing on the other end.

"Is that sweet Kevin?"

"It is. I just finished feeding him."

"I need to come to see him again soon."

"Want to come over now?"

"I'm on my way."

Minutes later, I was holding Kevin and waiting for a cup of tea to brew. Ashley was playing on the floor nearby with a couple of animals. This was one of those favorite moments.

"Can I just say for the millionth time how glad I am that you talked me into moving here?" I looked down at the baby's round face, "I was so lonely in New York. All I did was work, work, work. You were the only reason I did anything else."

"And I'm still doing it because I know you have a couple of articles due, right?"

"I do." I blushed. "You know me too well."

"You say it like it's a bad thing."

We laughed.

"So, I can't believe Gene offered me the magazine. It's a dream job."

"You will be so good at it, but what does this mean for where you live? Work?"

"I'm staying here without a doubt. I'm considering running it from both locations. I'll slowly move the headquarters here, but I haven't decided yet about printing. I'm going to discuss it with Gene but will also research cost, and especially carrier cost as we'll have to ship things back and forth if I do that."

"Still a lot of details to figure out."

"There are." I looked down at Kevin's face again. He was sleeping peacefully. "But I wouldn't miss days like this."

"Yeah, these days are special." She reached over and softly touched her five-month-old baby's head. He smiled in his sleep.

"Aw." We said in unison.

"Oh, you heard that Beth is pregnant again?" I asked.

"I hope this is the one. She has had too many lost."

"Yes, and I can tell it is really taking a toll on them both. Wade used to be such a jokester and always quick with a smile. Now he is so distracted and is working long hours."

"It's heartbreaking."

We continued chatting about neighbors and the town in general. That is a small-town for you, always sitting around gossiping about the good, the bad, and the ugly.

Over the next several weeks, I had many phone calls with the Butlers as we discussed details and made arrangements for their trip. As there weren't many hotels in the immediate area, I had offered them to stay in my house and offered to pick them up at the airport.

They only took me up on the offer of staying with me, but they planned to rent a car. I was waiting on them now. I kept pacing to the front window and then back to the kitchen. I didn't want to be hovering too much, but I couldn't help it. I would be seeing my mentor and friends after far too long.

I heard a car door, so I jogged to the front door, arriving at the same time as the Butlers stepped onto my porch.

"Welcome! I'm so happy to see you both." I hugged Marie first and then Gene.

"We are happy to see you as well," Marie said.

"Come in. Can I help you with anything?" I asked, reaching for Marie's bag.

"Oh, thank you, dear." She didn't fight me from taking it.

I lead the way to the guest room. I had them set up in the second one as the first was for my nieces and nephews. I had kept it childlike, mainly because I would have Denise Ann again this summer.

With this new job, I didn't know if I would have as much time for her, but I would try. She could stay with Frannie if I had to work, something I had already discussed with Fran. She loved the idea and said Denise could come over anytime, even if I didn't have to work.

"You have a lovely home," Marie said.

"Thank you." I set her bag down. "The bathroom is next door. There are towels, soaps, and everything else you need in there. Extra blankets are in this dresser, and extra pillows are on the top shelf in the closet."

"Perfect," Gene said.

"I'll let y'all get settled, and I will go fix you cold drinks. The kitchen is back down this hall towards the front door, and then straight back."

I left them and went to get some iced teas poured. I also had some cookies from Mary's Bakery. I would normally love to bake them, but I thought it would be nice to offer a local favorite.

"Oh, this is a nice room too." Marie said, coming in. "Gene is going to lay down a moment. I think the trip took a lot out of him. He won't admit it, but he is getting old."

"I understand." I laughed. "Here, I have some iced tea and some cookies from the local bakery."

"How lovely." She selected an oatmeal cookie, "These are my favorite."

She took a bite and gave a slight moan, "Oh, sorry, but these are amazing. You are going to have to take me to this bakery."

"Happily. It is run by the sweetest mother-daughter team."

"I love that." She took another bite, "So, are you excited about taking over the magazine?"

"I am. I have so many ideas."

"I can't wait to see how it all goes for you, and I am so happy that we can pass this to someone who understands it and will continue our vision."

We continued to chat and laugh until Gene woke an hour later. We had moved to my den just off the kitchen by then.

"Ah, I needed that nap." Gene said, joining us, "What did I miss?"

"Nothing much, just chatting with our girl here," Marie said, kissing his cheek.

"Well, I don't know about you ladies, but I am starving. What restaurants do you have around here?"

"We have a few. There is a wonderful diner then there a Mexican place and a barbecue joint, and finally, we have an Italian place that just opened. I have been once, and it was delicious."

"Let's go to the Mexican restaurant." Gene looked to Marie.

"Yes, I'm good with that."

"If you give me directions, I'll drive." Gene offered as we stood to leave.

"No problem."

The restaurant was a hit, and Rosa, our waitress, was a sweetheart. She had just married and was pregnant with her second child. Her mother, Carmen, was the chef and owner.

"Everything was wonderful as always, Rosa. Please let your mother know." I said as we were preparing to leave.

It was a wonderful reunion with my friends, and by the end of the week, I had quit my job and became the owner of Groove Magazine. I would make a trip soon to New York, and then I'd start working on shifting the business.

Chapter Thirty-Six: June 1978

I was on my third day back in New York City. It felt like a foreign country to me now, yet so familiar. I knew all the streets, the restaurants. I even knew many of the same faces on the road.

Of course, I had to stop in and see if Ms. Doris was still working at the Red Diner.

"No, sadly, she passed away. A few months ago." The waitress, who I didn't know, told me, "I started right after."

"Oh, I'm sorry to hear that." I tried to hide my disappointment and sadness. But, I still ordered my lunch, a pastrami sandwich with their homemade chips, "And, can I get an extra pickle with that?" I had to in honor of my friend, Frannie.

"Yep. Coming right up."

Now back at the office, I had a meeting with Bert and Sally. I was so glad to see that the dream team still worked here. Of course, none of the typists were the same, but that was expected. Jan was still working in the personnel department, but it had grown to three people. Marty, the boy who had collected our copy, got promoted to the printing supervisor.

The agenda for all my meetings, especially with Sally and Bert, was to let them know my plan to move things to Houston and ask if they were willing to move. I didn't know what to expect, but I was prepared for the worst. I had no plan if things didn't go the way I hoped, but I really wanted the two of them working for Groove as long as possible. I was willing to negotiate just about anything.

"There's the dream team. I'm so glad to see both of you." I said as they entered my office.

"We're happy to see you as well," Bert said through pursed lips. Yikes, that didn't seem happy to see me.

They sat on the edge of the seat. They sat ramrod still and didn't immediately start speaking, which I found odd. I knew in that instance that this wasn't going to go well.

"Well, I'll get right to the point. As you know, I've taken over from the Butlers, and I'm now the owner of Groove." I paused as they shifted in their chairs, "Since I live in Texas now, I am hoping to move at least part of the business there and maybe overtime the entire operation."

They looked at each other and had a secret conversation, or at least that's what it looked like. It was just a second before they looked back at me and waited for me to continue.

"I'm here to ask if you would both be willing to relocate to Houston with me."

"And if we don't?" Sally asked.

"Well, I guess I will figure out a way for us to conference between Houston and New York."

"Wait? You aren't firing us?" Bert said, almost falling out of his chair.

"No, is that what you thought?"

"Yes!" They blurted out at the same time.

"I thought you were both going to quit, but I definitely don't want to lose either of you."

We all laughed when we realized how wrong we all were.

"So, would either of you consider moving?"

"Well, since we thought you were firing us, we hadn't even talked about or thought what would happen if you asked us to move."

"Think about it and get back to me. I'm in town until Saturday." I said and then dropped my hands on the desk with a sigh, "I really want you both to stay on. You gave a kid a chance years ago, which I will forever be thankful for, but I want to continue to learn from you both for as long as possible."

"Great. We are looking forward to it as well." Sally said.

"We are so happy you are back," Bert added.

They left, and I got back to work. I met with all the employees to offer many of them the same deal. If enough moved, it would make the transition easier.

Next up, I met with Marty so we could discuss the printing. I needed ideas on how to best work in two locations, even for a limited time.

"It's so good to see you, Caroline."

"It's so good to see you as well."

"You know what's funny. The typists come and go, I would see many faces in a day, a week, but you, I remembered. You always said hi or smiled at me, even when you were busy. Not many did that."

"Aw, you are sweet. That made my day." I smiled, "Well, as I had mentioned to you earlier, I will be moving most of the departments to Houston, and I wanted to discuss how the printing might work. So my first question and concern is how it will work if we have all the copy and layouts in Houston and your team is here. Do you mail it overnight?"

"Yes, we could do that, or what I was thinking is we would work a month ahead."

"Hm, that's an idea. I hadn't thought of that. So, in August, where we normally get October's together, we would be doing November."

"Yes, that gives us more time for delays in geography."

"I like it." I made a few notes, "See, I knew I asked for your opinion for a reason."

It was such a simple solution. I wasn't sure how I had overlooked it, but there were so many moving parts, and I would depend on everyone to help me.

"I got a few brain cells up here." He chuckled.

"I know we aren't quite ready to move the printing department yet but have you thought about if you would move too?" I had already had this conversation with him and had given him time to think about it.

"I have, and I would."

"Oh, that's wonderful. It makes my life easier."

"I have nothing here but this job."

That made me a little sad for him. He wasn't a bad-looking man, though not my type. I liked them a little taller and beefier, but he was sweet.

"Well, Houston is a large area, but I will say I found what I was looking for in Glenn Lake. You should consider it when you move."

"I will look into it."

We wrapped our meeting shortly after. I met with the rest of the employees before meeting with Sally and Bert once again.

"I spoke with my husband, and he is good with the move," Sally said first.

"I'm not married, so I'm free to go wherever I like. I'm in. Let's go to Texas." Bert said, adding a yee-haw at the end.

"Well, alright. I'm so excited for this."

"We are too." Bert beamed.

"We are ready to help with anything that's needed," Sally added.

"It's going to take a lot of teamwork as we try to relocate most of the company and still make our printing deadlines. Plus, we are going to be introducing a longer lead time."

I explained the process Marty and I had developed and our plans.

"This sounds like a lot upfront, but I think we can do it," I said as I finished explaining it to them.

"I think it can work," Bert said but looked to Sally for her thoughts.

"Agreed, and while it sounds like a lot of work in the beginning, I think the end result will be good."

It took us nearly a year, but in the end, we moved the entire company, including printing, to Houston. We made all our deadlines and grew our readership. It was a lot of sleepless nights, lots of travel, and many missed meals and friends, but we all agreed it was worth it.

Chapter Thirty-Seven: Present Day

There was a knock on the door that snapped me out of my emotional walk down memory lane. I dabbed at my eyes, stood smoothing the front of my skirt before answering the door.

"Oh, Mandy, hello." I gestured for her to come in, "What a nice surprise?"

"Mama said you seemed a little down when she picked up the kids. So I just wanted to check on you." She frowned at me as she stepped in, "Have you been crying?"

I patted my eyes with the tissue again.

"Oh, just looking through old photos. There were some sad moments mixed in. But, you know a little rain to go with the sunshine."

I smiled and tried to keep my tone calm and steady, even though I felt a lump forming in my throat again.

"Do you want to talk about it? I'm a great listener. Just ask Mrs. Wills or Mrs. Dailey." She flashed me her beautiful Mandy smile, and it made my heart melt.

For whatever reason, my little Andrew hadn't lived but only those few days, and I never had other children. However, I realized Mandy was put in my life for a reason. Maybe to fill my life with love, joy and renew my faith.

"Oh, Mandy, I wouldn't even know where to start." I exhaled, not realizing I had been holding my breath.

"I'll make us some tea, and you can start at the beginning. Take it slow, and we can stop whenever you want."

We went to my kitchen. I watched as she started the electric kettle to heat the water and then selected her favorite teacups from my pink floral set. While the water heated, she placed an Earl Grey tea bag and a bit of sweetener to each.

I looked around my kitchen. The place had changed only slightly since I bought it all those years ago. I still had my cherry wood kitchen table, and it held so many memories of dinner parties, game nights, and sharing cups of tea with some of my favorite people.

"Before I start, you should grab us a couple of those chocolate chip cookies and a box of tissues. We'll need both." I laughed and then moved into my living room to retrieve the photo box with my most sensitive keepsakes.

She brought over the teacups, and I placed the box on the table, took a deep breath, and then started.

"Once upon a time, there was a man named Walter Franks. He was the love of my life."

I showed her the picture from our first date, the winter formal at school.

"This was the Winter formal. Wasn't he handsome?"

"He is." She studied his face, "Wow, Ms. Graham, I had no idea."

"I know. Only Frannie and Norm know about him, even though they never met him."

We flipped through picture after picture. It felt so good to share him with her. She was such a huge part of my life, and now at 18, nearly 19, she was in a good place with her life and was ready to hear about my struggles. To this point, she had been too young and had troubles of her own.

I reached into the box for the small yellow envelope with the most precious pictures and one soft yellow blanket.

"And these ... these are hard to look at and harder to share." I passed it to her feeling the lump in my throat grow, and tears form once again in my eyes.

She opened it and gasped, her free hand covering her mouth.

"You had a baby." She flipped through the few I had, the only proof that I had created life. They were over 50 years old, and it had become harder to believe it really happened.

"His name was Andrew Walter Franks. He lived for just a few days, but those were the most precious days. He was ... perfect." I picked up one of the pictures. I stared at his sweet, tiny face. "He had fought hard."

"I'm sorry." She squeezed my hands but didn't push for more information. I had always liked that about her. She was patient and thoughtful. It made this easier to talk about.

"Thanks. It was a long time ago."

"That doesn't mean it wasn't important or that the pain ends."

"Mandy, you are such a dear."

I pulled out a stack of pictures showing my first few months in New York City, so I told her about our move and my life with Walter.

"I hadn't even thought to be scared of the experience. On the contrary, I was naive, happy, and in love."

"It looks like you had a fun life. Is this where you worked at the fashion magazine?"

"It was." I dug through the stacks, "Here."

It was pictures of a few of my friends, including Gene and Marie Butler. I then told her how I got my job at Groove.

"And I was pouting in the diner when I started talking to a stranger next to me. Next thing I know, he is offering me a job."

"That's crazy!"

"He was the nicest man, and we stayed friends for years. Unfortunately, he passed away, gosh, 15 years ago. His wife Marie passed about five years ago."

"I'm sorry to hear."

I shrugged. They had lived long, wonderfully beautiful lives and had changed my life in so many ways.

"Is this Mrs. Dailey?" She asked me.

I peeked over at the picture she was holding. It was Frannie and me not long after we met. We had gone to a bar to listen to the Coleman Trio.

"It is. She dragged me out that night, and I was glad she did."

"Who is the other lady with you?"

"Oh, wow, Ms. Doris. She used to be a waitress at a diner we went to for lunch." I looked at her familiar face and crooked smile. "I used to want to be her when I grew up."

"Did you?"

I thought about her question. Doris had been thoughtful and spunky, chipper, and friendly. It might have just been a diner, but I had seen her buy meals for the homeless or the down on their lucks. She worked harder than people half her age.

"You know, I'd like to think I did."

She smiled at me. "So, what do you miss most from living there?"

"I miss the pizza. Oh, and there was this one coffee shop that had the best pastries."

"Better than Mary's bakery?"

"In my memory, they are, but in reality, probably not." I winked at her.

We then moved to my family pictures. My father and mother were both gone. Larry had passed away six years ago and his wife Mary Jane a year ago. So it is just me, Karl and Dean left. Along with both of their wives. Karl had lost a son to cancer, and Dean has lost both his children.

But the memories of all those family Holidays were frozen in these pictures.

"You've met Denise." Mandy nodded, so I continued, "She and Andrew would have been roughly the same age. Sometimes it's hard to see her and not wonder about him. I have other nieces and nephews, but she was the one closest to his age."

"I can only imagine what that must be like." She squeezed my hand then grabbed a new tissue with her other hand.

I held up a few special pictures of my mother. I missed her so much even to this day. I knew I would until the day I died.

"My mother is probably the reason I loved fashion so much. I might not have ever really learned to sew, but I understand fabrics, colors, and textures."

"You are always so well dressed. I've always admired your fashion sense."

"Aw, thank you, dear." I smiled, "I always miss my mother at Thanksgiving too. She made the best pecan pie. I have her recipe but have not been able to replicate it quite right."

"It was probably her love, more than the recipe."

Mandy was so profound. I stared at her for a second as I thought of what she had said.

"You are probably right. My mother had a lot of love for her family and friends. Always wanted the best for them."

"Like you."

A few fresh tears spilled from my eyes, and I quickly dabbed them. "You are truly the sweetest. I'm so blessed to know you."

I continued my stories for her. We laughed. We cried, but in the end, I was so relieved to have told someone.

"Ms. Graham, wow. I don't know what to say. I knew bits of your past, but I'm so glad you shared this with me." She picked up one of the pictures of a tiny Andrew. She stared at him. "He would have been a lot like you and probably like you said Mr. Franks was, a fun-loving, thoughtful person."

My heart tightened at her words. That is what I pictured him like as well, but I never had anyone verbalize my own private thoughts. It helped my heart to heal just that much more.

"Thank you. I think he would have been like that too, and probably a bit of a jokester." We laughed, "Can I tell you a secret?"

"Yes, of course."

I knew I could trust her not to judge or share, so I felt comfortable telling her.

"It's going to sound awful, but I used to struggle with how on earth your fourteen-year-old mother was given a healthy child, you, and I didn't and couldn't."

"Oh, that's not awful. You're allowed to feel how you feel. Plus, I have often wondered about that myself, how she had me and how I was never taken away from her. Yet there were so many couples that wanted children."

"Aw, I didn't know you felt like that either."

We stay in silence for a moment, each thinking. She broke the silence first.

"Well, I should get home, but I'm so glad you shared this with me, all of this."

But, before she left, and in typical Mandy fashion, she cleared our teacups and then helped me pick up the pictures.

I gave her a hug before watching her walk down my sidewalk and then up her driveway. She paused at her front door, giving me a wave.

I turned back into my house. I felt lighter like a weight had been lifted.

I hadn't realized until today that Mandy and her siblings, but mostly Mandy, weren't given to Becca for her but for me. They healed me and filled a void I hadn't realized was still empty. It explained so much of the past eighteen years of watching and helping and loving that girl.

That night I dreamed of Walter and Andrew. They were together, father and son. It was the first peaceful dream I'd ever had with them. Usually, my dreams were watching Walt being killed, and of the moment, I held Andrew as he passed.

Tonight, we were a family having a picnic. Father and son playing catch, and me laughing and watching from the dappled shade under an old oak tree. They came to join me, and we talked, ate, and laughed together.

When it was time to go, Andrew begged me to stay, to join them.

"Oh, my sweet boy, it's not my time yet. I can't stay, but I will see you soon. I promise."

THE END

Before you go: If you loved Caroline's Story, be sure to visit my website to sign up for my newsletter (if you haven't already) and to stay up to date on new releases and other bookish things.

When signing up, you will receive **Chef Jessica's Alphabet Soup Recipe** as a free gift. I have "had" it; it is yummy. (Okay, so obviously, it is my recipe, but still, I recommend it!)

Continue to the next section for this book's recipe!

Also, check out my other books! You can find links on my website.

www.ejwheltonwrites.com

Author note:

Thank you for reading Caroline's story. This was a true labor of love and has taken me longer than I had planned to write, but I wanted it to be a beautiful story and tribute to friendships.

I do have more plans in Glenn Lake and the Finding Herself series, though the next book may take some time to get ready for you. I think it will be worth it.

To give you an idea my plans are to give you Kate's story. If you remember she is Mandy's best friend and Olive's mother in Mandy's Story. It will be her story of escaping an abusive husband and starting her new life in Glenn Lake far from him, but is it far enough?

After that I am thinking I'll tell Claire's Story. She is Mr. Dixon's granddaughter and an employee of Mandy's. She drops out of college, but nobody knows why.

Then I have stories planned for Frannie, Mary, of Mary's Bakery, Ashley, Denise Ann, Rosa, Joyce who has not been introduced yet, Stephanie and many, many strong, wonderful women of Glenn Lake. At times, their partners or supporting characters may chime in, but most will be here solo telling their story.

Again, thank you for reading Caroline's Story. Until we visit Glenn Lake again, take care and make the best of every day.

For more information about this and my other work, please visit my website:

www.ejwheltonwrites.com

9 781956 069105